Leo Stone.

An abandoned child who could transform his body into the shape of a dog.

Fifteen years later, looking for answers.

WHAT AM I?

Unfortunately, he has found out.

And now he's running for his life

Other Titles by Pam Uphoff

Wine of the Gods Series
starting with Outcasts and Gods

The Directorate Series
Starting with Directorate School

The Lawyers of Mars
Fancy Free
Time Loop
In the Rift

Writing as Zoey Ivers

The Barton Street Gym

Chicago

Atlantis+

Fantasy:

Demi God

Stone

Pam Uphoff

Iron Ax Press

Chapter One

Freeway to Death
Or from, hard to say until you arrive

My paws hurt.

Didn't matter if I walked on the dry brittle grass of the verge, or the rough pavement of the shoulder. Too tired to Change. Too stubborn to quit.

If I had any sense I'd walk out into traffic and end it all. Death behind me and . . . nothing to walk forward into but a slower death than I'd dealt out to those back there. I had set out to find out what I was . . . and the answer was unthinkable.

I turned my head enough to see the cars and trucks coming up behind me. Not many, all going quite fast. I put my head back down and limped on.

Not just because of the paws. I heal fast. Maybe because of what I am. I'd lain unconscious for . . . maybe a day? After the fight. All the cuts and bites had healed on the surface, but there was a lot still going on inside. Especially in the hip joint. Damn near lost a leg.

Another car passed me, swerved to try and miss some trash on the road, ran right over it. Tossed it in the air. It clanged down a dozen feet away, then I could hear the thump, thump, thump of a flat tire. The car slowed and pulled over to the shoulder, a quarter mile down the road.

Another poor sod, dead on the road, going through the motions.

Well, no.

This was a pissed off blonde woman, kicking her car and glaring at the tire. Full of life, throwing her hands in the air and stomping around to pop the trunk of the car and start pulling stuff out.

By the time I limped up there was a pile of three suitcases, boxes, bags . . . nothing that smelled like food, unfortunately.

She stopped long enough to eye me, then turned back to the trunk to pull out a tool kit.

I flopped into the narrow bit of shade the biggest suitcase offered and watched her pull out the jack, the spare . . . So much energy, so much emotion. So alive and so real.

I closed my eyes. And "saw" with that faint sense, not quite sight but . . . the woman was a ghostly aura darting about. Nothing like the sick green of those people . . . my people.

Another car pulled over, stopped. Another faint white aura. I opened my eyes.

A man getting out of a bright red sports car. Grinning. "Hey Honey, need some help?"

Not one of the good grins. He swaggered up and loomed. "I can help you, if you're nice . . . "

I hadn't meant to growl. But I was careful to not limp as I got up to stalk closer.

The guy stopped. I'm a very large dog.

The woman smiled. "No thanks, I've got this."

The man eyed me, shrugged, and walked back to his car. Slammed the door.

I watched carefully, but he didn't try to run me down when he drove off.

"Huh." The woman eyed me. "Thanks, pup. Pity you didn't wait until after he'd changed the tire, though."

She leaned over and looked at the tags clipped on the twisted fabric around my neck. "Stone, eh? And a

3

phone number . . . 404? Isn't that an Atlanta area code? You're a long way from home, Stone."

I wagged my tail and limped back to the shade.

"So am I. Why the hell my sister moved to Phoenix . . . eh, love. At least *she* found a good one." She changed the tire with no more than a few curses, loaded everything back into the trunk and offered me a lift.

I accepted.

Chapter Two

On the road again

Having a big old dog along for the ride was kind of nice.

"It's less lonely with *something* alive to talk to." Rachel Bell shrugged. "Not that I talk to myself. I just think too much. Well, all right. I talk to myself. All the time."

From the back seat of the car, the thump, thump of a tail wag.

"And I need to stop thinking. Dominic wasn't even really a boyfriend, so it's not like any big deal he started dating Helen. We just . . . liked the same movies, went out to dinner a couple of times. But I bought the tickets and he bought the dinner, so it wasn't like real dating. I only kissed him once."

Tail thumps in reply.

"Gawd, I sound like a whiney high schooler. Anyway, the company folded, and my job with it, so my sister wanting me to come stay with her in

Phoenix . . . is timely. She said I should go back to college. Good plan. Maybe. I hated it. I made it through the first year and couldn't stand it any longer.

"But ugh. Receptionist. Pretty doll. Assumed to have no brain. Not to mention morals. Why didn't I get out of Nashville years ago, like Nichole?"

"Woof?"

She grinned. "You're a pretty funny dog. Did someone just dump you in the desert? I can't imagine why, unless you're not housebroken?"

That woof sounded indignant.

"So, Stone? What do you say we stop in Flagstaff to get the tire fixed, gas up and get some food? Then we'll head south for Phoenix." She shot a glance over the seat at the big dog. "Getting you into a hotel may be interesting. Maybe I'll just catch a few winks in a rest stop or something."

Thump, thump, thump.

"So, you understand 'food' do you?"

Thump, thump, thump.

Rachel found herself grinning for the first time in days. "Yep. Moving to Phoenix is an excellent idea. Especially with a big dog."

Thump, thump, thump.

6

The first garage she stopped at was happy to fix the flat.

She offloaded the luggage again, snagging the pull strap from the big suitcase for a makeshift leash. She bought a bottle of water from a vending machine, snagged a styrofoam cup beside the coffee machine, and sat on the footlocker in the shade. She unscrewed the cap on the bottle of water and poured some of it into the cup.

"Thirsty, Stone?"

"Woof!"

He made a bit of a mess on the sidewalk, but he drank pretty much all of it. Then the dog just laid down beside her until the car was ready.

"Let's find a place with a drive through, then we'll get back on the freeway." She figured Stone was good for three hamburgers. And two bottles of water.

She drove on down the highway to the first rest stop, to eat.

Where Stone limped out into the desert to dig a hole and take a dump. Bury it. Limp back.

"Well, that was certainly handy. I thought only cats did that . . . I suppose someone trained you, but it'd be a bit hard on the lawn or the flower beds. I hope Kris isn't an avid gardener." Rachel unwrapped the first burger, and handed it to him. He bit it in half, swallowed half with a couple of chews and scarfed the half on the sidewalk just as fast.

"Slow down, Pup. you don't want to get sick." She unwrapped hers and took a bite.

Of course I can't keep him. One, he belongs to someone, and two, I haven't the faintest idea if Kris likes dogs. What if he's a cat person?

"You know, Stone, I've only met my brother-in-law once, when I went to their wedding. I really don't know him at all."

"Woof?" Big begging eyes shifting between her and the bag of burgers.

She snickered. "Ham. You ought to be in the movies."

She unwrapped another burger and handed it over. "I may have to get a job quick and move out."

She unscrewed the cap on the bottle of water . . . "Oh dear, we have a logistics problem." But yesterday's fast food glass was under the seat and she poured the water in.

He drank it all. And inhaled his next burger.

"Typical dog."

8

"Woof?"

"Sorry, that's it." She popped the last of her own in her mouth and opened the back door for him. Shifted the front passenger seat all the way forward and reclined it as far as it would go, which wasn't very far.

Stone turned around and laid down, resting his head on the front seat headrest.

"That's about the right height for you, isn't it? Well. Let's hit the road."

An hour and a half later she was yawning, and glad to pull over at another rest stop. She parked in a far corner of the parking lot and looked worriedly at Stone. "Stay. I'll be right back and take you for a walk. *Stay.*"

She trotted over to the ladies for important personal reasons . . . and came back out to find Stone crouched on the ground facing two men who were plastered to the wall.

"Lady? Is this your nice doggy?" A nervous smile from the nearest fellow.

"Gentlemen? Is this the men's room that I have accidentally wandered into?"

She walked out, double checked the sign.

Definitely the ladies' room. No apology needed. "Come Stone."

From her car, she watched the men exit and rush off to the far side. She heard a car start, and drive away. Heaved a breath of relief.

Stone trotted off into the darkness, returned a few minutes later, and climbed in the back seat.

Rachel climbed behind the wheel, with a sigh. "I'll just relax, rest my eyes for a minute, then we can get out of here. Meet this brother-in-law of mine. Heck, it's been three years since I've seen my sister. Five since we lived in the same house. I was sixteen when she moved out, right out of college, got a job offer . . . fell in love . . . married. We don't hardly know each other as adults, you know? I really hope we still like each other. I was kind of a pest, as a kid." She sighed. "And Mom and Dad sold the old house and bought a condo on a golf course and strongly hinted that the guest room was for guests. Not a daughter who'd dropped out of college."

She leaned to scratch the dog behind the ears. "You're a good listener, Stone."

She leaned her head back and closed her eyes.

Chapter Three

Werewolf wannbes in New Orleans

"Werewolves?" Senior Special Agent Kristjan Kovac shook his head. "The Forty-eight gang thinks they are actual shape changing werewolves?"

The head of the Louisiana FBI nodded. "The kids bragged, and laughed when the cops told them to stop being so stupid. They could only be charged with vandalism. No ID, but they claimed to be sixteen—and looked it—so the judge turned them loose. They'd sent in DNA to help identifying them, too late to find the boys. The preliminary results—forty-eight chromosomes—meant nothing to them. But we get notified of any such results, and duplicated the genetic analysis, and the comparisons. At least, with the new tests we get results in a week. These came in yesterday."

Kris looked back at the photographs of the two boys. Five foot eight inches. Light hair, wiry build. Sharp boned faces with a strong family resemblance.

"What are they taking to give them delusions of being werewolves?"

The other man, who'd done the footwork, shook his head. "The lab said they were clean. We figure the Forty-eights are playing games because of the dog bites on some of the bodies. Trying to scare their rivals. We're looking—again—for large vicious dogs."

Kris snorted. "Faked, using dog teeth in some sort of crushing mechanism. Otherwise we'd have found canine DNA in the bites. And feline DNA in the claw marks." *And a damn good thing we've managed to keep a lot of the details quiet! Much better that they be known as a vicious drug gang. Or a satanic cult. Which might actually be true, but whatever they are, we need to find them.*

"True." The district head tapped one report. "The detailed DNA results are interesting. The boys', well, putatively young men's, extra chromosome pair is the same as all the rest of the gang's. And the same damned Y chromosome. Of the rest, lots of overlap, between the two of them and with the samples from the various rape-murder scenes. They aren't the rapists, but they are family."

"And they're gone." Kris eyed the pictures. A

convex profile with the entire lower face thrust a bit forward, the dental arc prominent in a long heavy jaw with a long narrow chin. Light brown hair, almost blond, short and straight in front, allowed to grow a bit at the nape of the neck and show a bit of curl.

"Good looking boys, but distinctive." One of the local men showed his teeth. "We're wondering if the whole family looks like this."

Kris raised his eyebrows. "Indeed. It would be nice to know what to look for.

Thirty-five multiple rape-murder scenes—the remains of over a hundred people found—spread out all over the country. Mind you, that's over a hundred year time period. And the first site was only discovered twenty years ago, before DNA analysis was sufficiently developed. But the old samples were kept, and the scene photos, descriptions, measurements.

Most serial rapists and murderers are loners. But with these people . . . gang rapes, torture, dismemberment . . . Cannibalism. The killing grounds very well concealed, only discovered accidentally, years or decades later. There are probably a lot more we haven't found.

I understand the Bureau not wanting to go public, to tell the public that all these various murders around the country are all related. That they have failed to find a single one of this gang or cult.

But if the public knew, would they help us find them?

He looked down at the chart. Each member of the gang had a letter and number designation. The letters from the scene where that specific DNA had first been found. And lines of relationships. Brothers, fathers and sons. Uncles. Grandfathers. Cousins. A hundred and fourteen individuals.

And now these two boys.

"The son of FL4. A possible cousin of PL1. So, one of the southern gang and one from the northeast. Only the fourth time we've seen individuals from different regions together. According to the records, your area's been free of their activity."

Four subgroups. Northwest, Southwest, New England, and the central East Coast. DNA suggests cousins, all descended from the same man. The Mitochondria are a bit more diverse. Three female lines produced eighty-two of the . . . werewolves. Nine other mitochondrial lines for the other thirty-two killers.

"Yeah. We're really hoping they're out-of-towners, visiting the Big Easy. You've got a big problem in Phoenix."

"Yes. Hideous mess. Worse than the Carolinas. I was in the Charlotte Field Office, when their third, the recent one, was found. They transferred me to Phoenix when they found the first mass grave, so they'd have an experienced investigator. We're up to three now." Kris grimaced. "If they hit again. For better or worse the two other sites we've found since then were even older."

"Yeah. We've all read up on the reports. So each group has a . . . spree every two to five years. And the most recent site is four years old. Right?"

"Right." Kris glanced from the head honcho to the agent who was working the case. "I'm surprised you could get the DNA profiles for juveniles."

A shrug from the agent. "The cops never ID'd them. They . . . sort of slipped into the system as being of uncertain age."

Kris nodded. "We keep trying to get permission to check juvenile records, and hitting a judicial wall. The new terrorism bill may help. Even though this is homegrown, and criminal."

The division head nodded. "Not that we have any idea if the gang includes its juvenile members in any of the rape-murders." He passed over a thumb drive. "Not that we couldn't have done this over the phone."

"True. I think my boss was hoping the police had a handle on the boys and I could get a look at them. The pictures will have to do." Kris shook hands around and headed for the airport.

I shouldn't have taken this assignment. Kept Nicole closer to her home, stayed local so I wasn't leaving her alone so often. I grew up in Tucson, missed the desert, wanted to get away from these mass killings. Well, I'm back in the desert, but haven't escaped the horrors of the Forty-eight gang. Six months and I've been out of town five times, now. Damn, investigating mass murders sure makes a man paranoid.

Southwest had a one-stopper to Phoenix, so he didn't have to change planes.

Nicole was waiting for him, worried. "Rachel isn't here yet. She called from Albuquerque last night and said she'd call if she decided to stop again. But she hasn't called."

"It's a long drive. She'll take breaks, and if she gets tired, she'll spend the night in Flagstaff. Your sister's got good sense." Kris hugged her, his own worries easing.

I hate leaving Nicole alone, so far from all of her old friends. Having her sister staying with us will be a big relief.

Chapter Four

Phoenix

"Almost there."

My blonde buddy sounded a bit tired. Well deserved, after driving probably four hundred miles with only a two hour nap in the small hours of last night.

I wagged my tail and sat up to look around. Phoenix was a sprawl of lights, tucked between mountains silhouetted by the rising sun. I'd slept through most of what had probably been spectacular desert, waking up periodically as the blonde woman mentioned something.

But if I was going to be here for very long, I really ought to sit up and take notes.

Like, which freeway exit led to wherever the blonde was going.

Turn here, turn there.

Hmm, hardware store, big computer center, big box stores on competing corners . . . Plenty of job opportunities, as soon as I acquired a few necessities. Pity I'd abandoned everything in Albuquerque. But I'd always known that could happen. Or that I might change unexpectedly.

And now a turn into a residential area, one last turn and then into the driveway of a big house.

The door of the house opened before the blonde had even turned the car off.

"Rachel! Yay! I was starting to worry."

"Oh, I got your message about going to pick up Kris so early, so I stopped and had breakfast. Hey Kris, long time no see!" The blonde—*Rachel! Finally, a name for her*—jumped out of the car.

The house was all adobe and red roof tiles. The woman who'd come out to hug my rescuer was red on top too.

"I thought you'd be here earlier."

My rescuer, Rachel, hugged the redhead. "Hey Nicole, I had a flat, had to stop and get it fixed and . . . well. Here we are." She cast a look back at me, in the rear seat.

"What is *that!*"

"That's Stone. He's lost, and well, he ran off a . . . person of uncertain intent when I was changing the tire. Don't worry, he's got tags, I'll track his owner down, I just couldn't leave him in the desert, he'd worn his pads down till they were bleeding."

"You always were soft hearted. Couldn't you rescue a smaller critter though?" The redhead peered at me.

"That's not a dog, that's a pony!" A man had come up behind them and now he was the one reaching to open the door.

"Very funny. Just because he doesn't look like one of your fancy police dogs . . . "

I eased out, putting my paws down carefully. Eight hours with hardly any walking had been nice, but not long enough to finish healing.

"Good Grief, he must weigh close to two hundred pounds. Mastiff or Newfoundland, by the size, crossed with, well, something with short hair, at least. Mostly."

They all looked at me.

"He's got a little bit of a curly ruff. He's not black like a Newfoundland." Rachel shrugged. "Do Mastiff's come in reddish brown? Maybe he's part Great Dane."

Nicole shook her head. "His ears are almost standing up. But he doesn't look at all like a German

Shepherd . . . "

Strictly speaking, I probably wasn't even partly canine. Nonetheless, I wagged my tail, sat down and offered a paw to shake. I needed more than a couple cheeseburgers to regain enough energy to Change, to . . . re-enter human society . . . somehow.

All three of them had nice white glows.

Not like . . . those people. Or even the hungry red tinge of those potential rapists at the rest stop. The sullen gray of my foster siblings.

Just . . . good honest people.

This looked like a good place to recuperate.

So the first thing that happened was I got hosed off, soaped down, and scrubbed. Really embarrassing. Not that it didn't feel good, but.

Oh well. I got a plateful of leftovers and a rug on the back porch and thought I was in heaven. The concrete patio had absorbed the heat all day, and felt wonderful as the sun set and the air cooled.

I could hear them chatting inside. Well enough anyway to piece things together. Rachel had lost her job, been dumped by her boyfriend and been invited to come and stay with her sister and her husband. This was some sort of temporary posting for the guy.

And they phoned the numbers on my tags. The first number wasn't in service, of course. I perked my ears and listened to the call to the vet.

"An old number . . . Oh, is that the Stone's huge brown dog? He must be . . . fourteen by now, a big dog like that I'm surprised . . . But he always was an odd dog—he actually had retractable claws like a cat. Harriet was so cute, a little old lady with a dog twice her size and so well behaved!"

The Stones, my foster family. Once they realized I wasn't *just* a little boy, they'd made sure I had the *other* set of vaccinations too. Just in case.

"Do you have their phone number? I found the dog in New Mexico."

I couldn't pick up all the rest. ". . . heard their son Leonard moved." And then loud and clear, "After they both died a couple of years ago."

I put my head down and stopped listening. I knew. I arranged their funeral, then their biological children tossed me out. "You're nineteen, you're an adult. Go live in the dorms if you're going to stay in college." And "Don't expect us to pay for it. Bad enough you conned Mother and Father into paying tuition while you freeloaded on their generosity."

Stanley and Harriet Stone. Wonderful people. Their kids, not so much.

So I was homeless before the only parents I'd ever known were buried. A backpack full of the bare necessities, a suitcase with everything else I could cram into it.

Fool that I was, instead of crashing at a friend's house and looking for a job, I'd decided to go find out what I was.

I didn't really remember much, from before the police picked me up, a naked boy, maybe five years of age, wandering the streets. There were places I could recall, with no memory of where they were. Names that rang a bell, things I dreamed. By then I'd accumulated quite a file of places to check, mostly from internet searches.

So I'd . . . just gone. And once the savings were gone, I'd picked up some work for a while, then moved on to the next place on my list.

Five years of searching, and I finally found them in Albuquerque.

And the next evening found myself out in the desert with a half-dozen shape-changing killers. And told them I wouldn't join them.

Chapter Five

Settling in

The dawn was spectacular.

Rachel dressed for running, and slipped downstairs. Nicole's new house was nice. Mid-sized with good sized rooms. One big room, not a formal living room, and a den. One dining room. No breakfast nook. She opened the back door and was greeted by a tail wagging oversized mutt stretching and limping over to her.

"Paws still sore, poor mutt? Well, I won't invite you out for a morning run yet, then. And I'll buy a bag of dog food today too. And find something to feed you in about half an hour." She rumpled his ears, and closed him out.

Nicole had given her a house key—she slipped it in her pocket and set out to explore the neighborhood.

She stretched and walked down to the corner. Ten houses on this little cul-de-sac off a straight road— good grief! Did they even number the little streets?

"Well, I won't get lost." She set off down the sideway, crisp cool desert air. It'd be a furnace by noon, but now it was nice. She picked up an easy pace and wound off into the winding subdivision streets. Judging from the exteriors, Nicole and Kris's house was large but not a standout in a neighborhood of nice homes. Desert landscaping predominated, the lawns looked dry and worn.

She got lost, found a numbered street, and loped home to the smell of baking pastries and coffee.

Stone wagged up to greet her.

"Is my sister trying to turn you into a house pet?"

Nicole's voice came from the kitchen. "He's house broken, and knows how to open sliding glass doors to go out when he needs to."

"The weird thing is he closed the door behind him. Both going out and when he came back in." Kris looked up from the newspaper he was reading in the dining room. "Have a nice run?"

"Yes! No humidity to speak of. Marvelous." Rachel stuck her head into the kitchen. "Can I grab a shower before that's ready?"

"Five minutes."

Her hair was still drippy when she returned to

sink her teeth into a huge cinnamon roll. "Mmm, delicious. Aunt Mudge's recipe?"

"Yep." Nicole eyed her stringy hair. "I didn't realize you'd kept up the running. There's some much more scenic places to torture yourself with. The Canal Trail or Murphy's Bridle Path. Or if you need a challenge, South Mountain Park. Or just keep running around the neighborhood, if you're not inclined to drive someplace to run."

"I'll check them out tomorrow." Rachel refrained from licking buttery fingers. Ignored the big brown eyes that were close to shoulder height. "Today I need to hit the store and buy some dog food."

"Woof?"

"No, I'm not going to start out feeding you cinnamon rolls. I expect it wouldn't be good for you. And I need to spruce up my resume."

Kris nodded. "Nicole mentioned you might try college?"

"I'll look into it, but I don't want to borrow too much. So I need at least a part time job. And search the internet for this Leonard Stone person while I still want to give his dog back to him."

Chapter Six

Sunday night at Walmart

A solid night's sleep, and another day off my feet, and I was back in working order. I waited until twilight, then trotted most of the way to the Walmart we'd passed after we'd gotten off the freeway. Then I ducked behind a sign and triggered the change.

Deep breathing to help fuel the energy used, a mindset of half self-hypnosis to control the pain . . . it only took about five minutes, but it always felt longer. I pulled the "collar" over my head and unrolled and untwisted a pair of black running shorts. Checked the pocket. A plastic bag with my drivers license, social security card, an ATM card to an account that was down to fifty dollars and, this time, almost two hundred dollars in cash.

Everything else I own is in the trunk of my car back in Albuquerque.

So. Time to shop.

Walmart, being what they are, late night shoppers are infamous for the odd clothing their customers wear. My bare chest and bare feet barely raised an eyebrow.

Two tee shirts, two pairs of jeans, a packet of tighty-whiteys, socks, running shoes. All cheap generics. $75 and I was ready to rejoin human society.

Well, maybe tomorrow morning, after another good night's sleep. And I'd probably have to sleep on Rachel's patio in dog form until I find a job and get my first paycheck.

I walked back to the Kovac's in human form, to get the muscles and tendons all stretched out properly. Almost three days in a sort-of-dog-form had let everything get hard and solidly into the size and shape of a dog. I really needed to spend more time human . . . and change regularly. I'd been slow and stiff to change, out in the desert.

Damn near got myself killed.

At least most of them had left once they had me tied up to that post.

"You kids take care of him. And clean up the mess." The oldest man had said. He'd left just two human-forms and two dog-forms arguing about how inventive they ought to be—and whether they freaking well ought to *eat* me!

The human shaped ones had sent the doggish ones off to collect firewood, and started dancing and . . . praying. Singing maybe. They'd raised . . . dust. It was only dust and smoke. And maybe they'd drugged me. It wasn't glowing. It *wasn't*! The fire, the setting sun, all creating an odd illusion. I'd already started changing, slipped my paws out of the ropes, and gotten most of the way out of my binding clothes before one of the men turned around and saw me.

I'd hoped to sneak away, run for it . . .

I shuddered, remembering the taste of blood in my mouth. Shut down the memory. I'd run away from Albuquerque. I'd escaped. They'd never find me again. I could live like a normal man.

I hope!

I got all the price tags and such off my new clothes and hid them in the bushes that filled the narrow side yard.

Then I rolled up my shorts, clipped on the dog tags and pulled it over my head and changed.

Laid down on my rug on the patio and snoozed.

***

Monday morning I alternately trotted and galloped along with Rachel. Exercise for her, learning the neighborhood for me.

Then they closed me in the laundry room so I wouldn't wander off while they went shopping.

I listened to them drive away before I changed. A quick shower would be good . . . I found a linen closet, and some towels that showed a bit of wear at the back. Surely they wouldn't miss them. I used Rachel's bathroom upstairs. I hesitated, then used Rachel's toothbrush.

Must not have bad breath for the job interviews!

And deodorant! I hope Rachel never finds out.

I looked carefully for peeping neighbors before I streaked for the bushes where I'd hidden my new clothes. This skinny unkempt space between house and fence was going to be handy. I hung my towel on a low branch to dry. Then it was time for a hike.

First a cheap tosser phone and set it up with a memorized credit card number. I wonder where my card is? I left my clothes and wallet behind in the running fight with the dog forms . . . That's going to be a problem. But nothing I can do about it until I have a paycheck and an address they can send a replacement to.

I filled out applications at three stores, and on the way out of the hardware store picked up a quick gig loading and unloading lumber for a nice lady who paid me twenty bucks and dropped me off at a corner store two blocks from home. Well, Rachel's home.

Uh, oh, cars in the driveway. I doubled back to the convenience store, bought deodorant, toothbrush and toothpaste . . . Then I changed in the bathroom. Trotted out on all fours with my collar back on, carrying everything else rolled inside the jeans. Shoes dangling, laces tying the package shut.

I ignored the "Hey!" from the clerk, shoved the door open and trotted away. I could hear Rachel calling me . . . I waited for silence and peeked around a corner and spotted her walking inside. I bolted down the street and jumped the fence into the bushes. Buried my clothes in dry leaves, then emerged, stretching and yawning.

"There you are! Good grief, you have got to be the laziest hound dog in existence. And how you got out of the house, I have no idea!"

I gave her my best doggy grin and wagged my tail

and got, drat, doggie treats, instead of leftovers. Urf, and she'd bought a big bag of dog food . . . *Well, I can deal with it for a few weeks.*

So I snoozed on a rug on the back porch, and in the morning I cleaned up under the faucet, dressed . . . and answered my phone. By noon the nice lady in the back office of the hardware store had hired me and I had acquired the purple shirt of a properly dressed employee of Handyman Central. Embroidered name tag ordered. All costs to come out of my first paycheck. "You can wear your jeans today, but you'll need to get khakis before you come to work tomorrow."

Then I had to hunt down an Allen Burton, my boss. Nice older guy, confident and friendly.

"So, lots of experience in other hardware stores, eh? I see you've moved around a bit."

Oh, guess he saw my application.

"Well, this is Jose Ortiz. You're going to follow him around and see how *this* store does things. Do what he tells you to do."

Jose grinned. "Pale palmaditas en la cabeza y frota tu barriga."

34

I patted my head and rubbed my stomach.

They both laughed and Mr. Burton waved us out.

I worked happily until closing time.

And hesitated . . . Only two miles to Rachel's home . . . free food and with luck I can use the shower before I go to work tomorrow . . . so long as I don't have to shock some poor vet.

I found a dark corner to change and trotted home. Got scolded, and shoved in the laundry room with a bowl of dog food and a bowl of water.

Drat.

Chapter Seven

A new kill site

The desert was littered with old gold mines. Just holes in the ground, abandoned a century or more ago, a hazard for hikers, a dangerous attraction for the curious.

"At least these are old." The Sheriff's deputy glanced over at the FBI forensics team, down the hill, some of them down the hole. "Surprised you boys are out for this."

Kris shrugged. "Frankly I doubt there's any connection to that kill site over in Pima County, and this is even older." He shrugged, as the Standard Response rolled off his tongue. "But all the conspiracy theorists love this stuff."

"Yeah, and with all the animals having a feast, it superficially resembles a massacre." Deputy Nunez eyed him sidelong. "Dismembered bodies . . . charring . . ."

"Yeah, keeps the forensic people in business. And

Coroners get a thrill at seeing something unusual."

Kris refused to meet his eyes. *That wide circle over there, with no older, taller brush . . . they'll find the filled in post holes for those five poles dropped into the mine. The fire pit.*

And once they get all the bodies out of the caved-in parts of the mine, there will be five female skeletons. First guess from the state of the forearm some stupid dog dug up and brought to his master to play fetch with . . . she died six years ago.

Four mass graves in Arizona. So far. Keeping it quiet isn't going to last much longer.

He walked out to the tarps where they were laying out bones, dried mummified flesh and skin covering many. But not all. *Cannibals. I'm just glad this is an old site. The three week old one at Forty Acre Rock was . . . gruesome.*

He shook his head and walked back.

"I remember being an idiot, like this. I was just luckier."

"Around here? I thought you were new."

"I grew up in Tucson, the bureau's sent me around to a few different field offices. Last year they threatened me with a transfer to DC, so I begged for

Arizona."

The deputy grinned. "And here I'd heard the J. Edgar Hoover Building was the goal of every agent."

"Well, yeah, if you can deal with politics, the cost of living, and the commute. Nicole was delighted that the next adventure in being married to me was going to be strange, exotic and not political." Kris glance at the deputy. "A bit of diplomacy when we tromp all over the locals' business, comes in useful, however."

That got a grin. "I'm a touch claustrophobic. I'm quite happy to sit out here in the sunshine and watch a pack of Feds risk their lives collecting what needs to be collected from a six-year-old tragedy. Underground, in a half collapsed mine."

Kris nodded. "When you put it that way . . . and for some reason I just haven't found a compelling reason to check out the collapse site up close and personal."

A snort from the deputy. "Well, I'll leave you high-and-mighty Feds to your tasks. I'm out of here."

Kris walked over to the broad circle of lower growth.

Agent Brad Cohen walked over to join him. "What's up?"

"From up there, I could see that this circular area has no tall brush. Once you're done with the bone retrieval . . . "

"We start the dance floor. You got it, boss."

"Dance floor. Well, I suppose it's as good a thing to call it as any." Kris shook his head. "You found five poles?"

"Yep. You betting on five victims?"

"Yeah. Damn. I can't figure these guys out. They aren't drug users, but there were traces at the more recent sites. Transporters, maybe? But they've never been ratted out. Not once in twenty years. Are they just regular guys with regular jobs who get together occasionally to satisfy their kinky urges? A *family* of several hundred perverts?"

"Genetic? Those extra genes messing up their socialization?" Cohen wrinkled his nose.

"And they're raised this way? Eh . . . A religious cult of cannibals is my guess." Kris looked back at the mine, where the guys below were handing up their latest finds.

"It's weird though, that there's never been a deserter, no one has ever talked. For all this time."

Chapter Eight

Sticker shock

"Good god! What happened to college tuition while I wasn't looking?"

Rachel looked over her sister's shoulder . . . "Yikes! I've heard that when the government stepped in with student loans the universities all decided the sky was the limit. But this is just flat out obscene . . . Uh . . . That's per year isn't it? Not per semester?"

She glanced the other way, and started laughing. "Looks like Stone's shocked too."

Nicole grinned. "Even shocked the poor dog, eh? Well, you don't have to worry about room and board. Let's check out the campus, see what it looks like."

Rachel nodded. "And then check out online classes. Because, yowch. And I'd better start looking for work, too."

"Woof!"

They cracked up laughing, then hunted around the internet a bit. Stone lost interest, and went and read the mail on the desk.

Rachel giggled.

Because really, it probably just smells interesting, but it looks so much like he's reading . . .

"All right, Stone. Back into the laundry room with you, and this time I'm going to make sure the outside door is firmly closed and locked. No, big begging brown eyes are not going to get you the run of the neighborhood. I need to find this owner of yours, or give up and admit I have a dog. And get a gate latch you can't work."

She checked the outside door. Locked. Jerked it. Definitely closed. Poor Stone was giving her the whole ears down, head down, sad dog slink. She hardened her heart and shooed the dog into the laundry room. Closed the door firmly.

Nicole was snickering. "That dog's a manipulator."

"I noticed. So let's go check out the campus, first, and then figure out where I'm going to get over twenty thousand dollars a year to attend college."

Chapter Nine

Off to work

A quick shower, dress and hike to Walmart for their cheapest pair of khakis, and I was ready for my second day of work.

I changed to the khakis in the men's room. Looked in the mirror . . . the running-shorts-collar and dog tags really didn't work with the purple polo shirt. I pulled them off and felt naked.

Don't be silly, you can leave them with your jeans, nothing's going to happen.

But they're the bare minimum I need to get going again.

I stuffed them in the pocket of the khakis and got to work.

Stocking shelves was kind of boring, but Mr. Burton was full of stories about the desert. Hunting, exploring the old gold mines, roaming the hills.

Maybe I could be a wild animal . . . who, speaking of hunting, hasn't a clue how to catch dinner. Never mind.

"My son never took to hunting." He sounded a bit sad. "But I've got two grandkids so far, maybe they'll like going out into the desert."

Then he sent me off to work, shifting sacks of fertilizer, with John Gardner, who griped the whole time about his child support payments to three ex-wives.

Five children. I wouldn't dare a single one. How did such an ugly fellow persuade three women to marry him? Red-faced and sweating, pocked complexion and shaved head. Tattoos. Beats me.

"And they're just snot-faced little monsters. It's not fair that I have to pay so much. Their mothers spoil them, no discipline at all."

Little monsters. What sort of monster am I? I really don't know anything about what I am that I didn't know already.

Oh wait. My blood relatives are cold blooded killers. All of them, apparently. Very large monsters. Dammit. I wish they'd have talked more, told me more before they decided it was time to kill me.

I could have used a lesson in weird biology, but all I got was talk about demons and sacrifices.

I heaved the last sack up to the top of the pile, and headed back to find Mr. Burton. I stopped and gave some ladies advice about lightbulbs, got volunteered to load lumber, bags of cement, learned the cash registers—virtually identical to ones I'd used before—then back to fetching things off tall shelves, mostly for people who seemed to know what they were talking about. All-in-all, a nice long work day. I walked home in the dark, stopped in a shadowed area to change, and trotted the rest of the way . . . where the guy—Kris Kovac if the name on the envelopes was right—was working over the gate latch, with both women observing.

Drat. I guess camping out here isn't going to work. Maybe I can squeeze out one more day, then start camping . . . somewhere that won't land me in the dog pound.

I slunk around, staying behind parked cars, got over the fence and into the other side yard to drop off my clothes, then jumped back over.

I trotted up behind them. Sat down and perked up my ears. "Woof!"

And grinned and wagged my tail as they jumped and cussed. At least Rachel laughed with me. It was enough to make me wish I was normal. Or had the nerve to risk . . . well, I mean, what sort of children would I have? No way was I brave enough to find out.

Not ever.

"Well, we might as well leave him in the backyard tonight. Then find out if he can still get out of the fence." Kris shook his head. "And I'll see if I can locate this Leonard Stone from Atlanta."

Good Luck! I haven't lived in Atlanta for five years now.

But . . . was that a gun peeking out from under his shirt as he leaned to pick up his tools? He didn't strike me as a criminal, nor the neighborhood as especially dangerous. So that left paranoid or . . . Well, not that perfectly ordinary people didn't carry guns, but . . . well, this was Arizona, not the Northeast where I'd lived for the last three years. Fewer gun laws, more snakes. According to the reputation of the Southwest as a whole.

But the other alternative was that he was a policeman. So maybe he could get information on Leonard Stone.

And he'd probably have access to info about what had happened last week.

Chapter Ten

Bodies in the New Mexico Desert

"The New Mexico State Police have found two bodies out in the desert. Preliminary cause of death dog or coyote bite injuries. No other indication that it could be related to the Forty-eights—victims are male, no dismemberment and so forth—but we're keeping an eye on it until the DNA results rule it out."

"More like drug gangs clashing. They keep pit bulls for guard dogs, and sometimes those huge cane corsos. Teach them to attack and maul." Steven Chen shrugged. "Bet they find gunshot wounds as well."

Nods around the table.

Brent Masterson was the Arizona District head. He glanced over at Kris. "Senior Special Agent Kovac has information on the new site. Kris?"

He told them all about the five new victims, the usual dancing floor. "I think I'm going to hate that name. But it's all been sent off to the national data base."

"Unfortunately, we have nothing new from New Orleans. Unfortunately the two boys, or young men, we don't have an age for them, were released due to their apparent youth and the minor charge. Long gone before they got the preliminary DNA results. Forty-eight chromosomes." Kris filled in the details.

They all studied the pictures again.

"I'm running them through facial ID, see if we can find some family members with police records. Cousins that look this much alike, I'm hoping there's a strong family resemblance. We need a break before they kill again."

Chapter Eleven

Job Hunt

"And please stay in the yard!" Rachel walked back inside, carefully locking the sliding glass door to the patio. "Right. Wish me luck!"

She scooped up her pile of resumes, tucked them into a file folder.

Nicole grinned. "Good luck! I ought to be out there looking too . . . but a paralegal married to an FBI Agent . . . I don't want to cause a conflict . . . and we'd like to start a family."

"So you're stuck in the house and bored to tears?"

"Meh. I do some stuff online, and tutoring at the high school. But . . . "

"It's not a glamorous law office?"

"Definitely not. It's . . . My actual job wasn't glamorous . . . and . . . I dunno. What do you do when you've got that college degree and then you find the job is boring, poorly paid, and a dead end?"

"You marry a handsome FBI Agent and move halfway across the country. Do you still paint? I remember the messes you used to let me make with your paints. I never did figure out how you made them behave and make the pictures you wanted them to be."

Nicole laughed. "You were so funny, you'd get frustrated . . . I haven't painted in years. You know what? I'm going to dig out those boxes of my art stuff, and see what I still have."

Rachel trotted out to her car, still parked at the curb. Right. I'll start at those offices and then check out the . . . umm . . . retail opportunities.

She eyed the cute guy walking down the sidewalk. Purple shirt? Must work for Handyman Central. Gee. Maybe I should apply there. It can't be worse paid than receptionist and has the advantage of working with guys with muscles. Scenic. But first I'll try those professional buildings off Seventeen.

Thirty-nine resumes handed over, half as many applications filled out, and only three brief chats with HR types, she walked the length of the big strip center filling out applications for the four stores that were hiring.

Four in the afternoon. I should go home and see if Stone hung around this time. She pushed the button to send her info to Electronics Inc, and walked back to where she'd parked, and drove down to the other end.

Hardware store or Captain Freeze? Not that I have the faintest interest in a job in a fast food joint, but a milkshake right now sounds wonderful.

Rachel opted for straight chocolate. *If this passes the chocolate test, I'll start trying their exotic flavors, one by one.* The inside seating area was over flowing with noisy overactive children. She walked outside where there were tables . . . all occupied. One guy sitting alone caught her eye and waved a hand at the chair across the table.

"I've got to get back to work, so I'll be out of your way in a second." He was wearing a purple shirt . . .

"Thanks. So, what is Handyman Central like to work for? I'm job hunting."

He's kind of cute. Distinctive.

"Well, I like it so far, but I've only been working here four days, myself." He popped the last bite of a burger into his mouth and started gathering up his wrappings and napkins. He glanced at a bare wrist.

51

"Drat, I hate not having a watch. Umm, Hi, I'm Leo . . ." His gaze froze, looking over her shoulder.

Rachel tossed a glance over her shoulder. Nothing alarming that she could see, but Leo was standing up and retreating.

"Good luck with the job hunt." And he was gone, down the sidewalk, nearly running.

Well . . . that was ego crushing. Not that I want to be movie star gorgeous, but I'm pretty good looking and made up for job interviews. He might have at least looked reluctant to go. Instead of terrified.

"Dear me. Have you been abandoned?"

Rachel looked back around. Blinked. If his hair was darker he could be Leo's twin.

She answered automatically. "No, we were just sharing a table. I guess I hit their busy time."

"The Elementary Schools let out half an hour ago. The next wave—teenagers—will strike anytime now." This one had a charming smile as he sat across from her. "I'm Devon Canis, I'm a regional manager for Fast Furniture."

"Rachel Ball, job hunter. Pleased to meet you." Rachel sucked down the last of her chocolate shake, smiled as she stood up, and walked back through the zoo inside to her car.

She looked over toward Handyman Central, then shook her head. "Doubt they need me. I'll apply there if I get desperate." She started her car and headed home. "And I actually spoke to two men today. Even if the first guy sort of fled in terror. I wonder what set him off?"

She grinned as her imagination went to work. "Spotted his evil twin and ran for it? Hmm, or maybe he's the evil twin?"

Chapter Twelve

Danger! Panic! Oh crap!

I plastered myself to the back wall of the restaurant and got my panic under control.

No adrenaline-rush-fueled-change allowed. Especially here in public in plain sight.

Deep breaths. Calm. Centered.

The emotional control I'd learned in Karate had really helped me to have a normal life. And I could feel that it was saving me again.

No change. Engage brain.

I had not seen one of them. I couldn't have.

I closed my eyes. The zigging high energy spots of children, the softer glows of adults. The bright clean glow of Rachel Ball . . . and the sickly greenish-yellow glow of one of them.

Walking up to Rachel.

I started feeling dizzy and cupped my hands over my mouth.

Don't hyperventilate! Pay attention! Did he see

me? Or did he approach Rachel because she's beautiful and sitting alone?

Oh God. It doesn't matter.

They claim to hunt and kill women.

I forced myself to calm down. Again. To watch as Rachel left. Drove away. And the nasty glow followed her. I'd never looked so far away . . . reached out . . . stretched to see Rachel turn up the little cul-de-sac the Kovak's house was on . . . and I saw the Bad Glow pause, then drive past, turn and pass the mouth of the cul-de-sac, again pause and then drive on.

They know where she lives.

I swallowed and tried to watch the . . . my fellow . . . *Hunters of Men, they called themselves.*

He passed the far side of the strip center without turning and kept going north . . . turned left, west, and drove beyond my ability to "see" him.

I let it go and opened my eyes.

Time to get back to work. And figure out how I was going to keep an eye on Rachel, and how to find *them.*

Figure out what to do.

***

I worked frantically the rest of the afternoon, and stayed until they closed the store. Found a dark corner to go all doggish, hid my clothes there, and headed out to track down the enemy.

North and then west. Even trotting along steadily, with a few sprints to cross streets, I was slow. He could have driven past Phoenix's city limits, through Peoria and Sun City and kept going.

But in Albuquerque they'd taken me first to a big warehouse in an industrial area. And they'd been recognizable regulars at that restaurant . . . and like me they must need to work and earn money.

I stopped to catch my breath, and close my eyes and reach way out . . . Rachel's house was a mile and a half from Handyman Central. So . . . in theory I had mentally followed that *Hunter* out this way two miles. So if I was one more mile past that and tried to find him . . . and failed . . . It was time to get moving. I could check every mile or so, until I got to Highway 60, then jog north a mile or so and work back a bit . . .

My third stop I felt something northwest and moved that direction.

Seven sickly glows from three houses.

I kept my distance and made sure my doggy eyes

were reading the street signs and house numbers right. Not that I got that close, but the numbers were jumping by fours, so I had a pretty good idea of their addresses. I limped more slowly back to the Handyman Central, detouring only to soak myself in a, probably malfunctioning, sprinkler system.

Closest to a bath I was going to get today. I was dry by the time I got back to the landscaped corner where I'd left my clothes. I curled up and slept under the bushes.

Chapter Thirteen

Tracking and Tall Tales

I woke before dawn, changed and got dressed before slipping out from behind the euonymus bushes and going in search of breakfast.

Donuts were the cheapest. I munched and watched the sun rise until Mr. Burton arrived to get things started. He let me clock right in and put me to work moving the eye catchers outside as they turned on the lights and unlocked the doors.

Excellent. I'll either rack up some overtime or I'll get sent home early. Either is a good idea, because my cash is getting pretty low.

I'll have to go back to the Kovacs' and eat dog food.

But that's also the best way to keep track of her, guard her.

***

I was getting a kitchen sink down from the top of the very tall shelves when I spotted Rachel chatting with Miss Nina, the head of the office staff. Was Rachel applying for a job here too?

It would make guarding her from those hunters a lot easier.

And it would make getting to know her, human-to-human, possible.

And that was almost scarier than my putative relatives. Because I'd never dared have a real girlfriend. Not even when I was a semi-popular member of the football team in high school. Oh, there'd been several girls I talked to regularly, but not *dated*. I'd outraged everyone by taking three girls to the prom. Well, they'd put their heads together and made a plan. They'd asked me to the prom. All three of them at once. We'd had a fun time and I'd kissed each one of them once . . . I was a pretty nerdy seventeen-year-old.

At twenty-four, more or less, since I didn't really know when I'd been born, things could get more serious and I really didn't dare.

I watched Rachel's blonde curls from my perch . . . and got back to moving boxes to find the one that inventory claimed was up here.

By the time I found it, Rachel was gone.

60

Stone

And at "lunch" which happened to occur at two in the afternoon for the times I was supposed to be working—my first paycheck.

Miss Nina smiled at my expression. "It's only for part of the week, and with the deductions for everything, well, the next one will be much bigger."

In as much as I had been wondering if I could afford lunch at all, this was very welcome. I had a good memory for numbers, so there was no trouble depositing the check in my old bank account, and getting a twenty in cash.

If I dared return to Albuquerque I'd have a checkbook, a computer, and a car.

Not to mention a futon and my own towels and dishes . . . I'd feel rich.

I suppose my wallet's out in the desert somewhere.

A chill ran up my spine. No. Either the police have it, or those . . . Hunters of Men.

Do I need to check the news? Have they found any bodies out in the desert? Surely at least one of them died.

I walked down the street from the bank. A

Mexican restaurant with a cheap lunch menu. Exactly what I needed. Then back to work, and after work . . . tracking.

***

I circled out from the houses I'd found. Only five of the Hunters were there, and I started working outward . . . but was still close enough to feel three others arrive at the houses I'd found.

They all moved then. Three fast clumps. Cars. Heading west.

I was northwest of them and ran westward, checked, damn all fast cars! They were northwest and moving . . . slowing . . .

I sprinted . . . got to highway 60 and realized they must be on it, two miles ahead of me. In slow rush hour traffic.

I settled down to a steady trot, and didn't lose them until they were past Peoria, with no indication they were going to stop.

At least there are no white glows in the cars. If they're going somewhere out in the desert, it's without a victim.

I turned around and started limping back. At least

my hip wasn't hurting. A little skin off my pads would heal fast enough. And another night of sleeping rough. Maybe I'd change back and buy dinner. Although I was hungry enough that even kibble sounded good.

No it didn't.

When I got back to my little nest in the bushes, I changed and dressed.

Checked my cash. Not enough to splurge, but a burger at the all night place would be just fine. I waited until there were no cars driving by and slipped out of the bushes and around the corner.

I sat outside and savored real human food . . . And looked up to find a man watching me. A Hunter.

Oh shit.

Oh . . . opportunity. Can I pass myself off as being from out of town? Ask questions?

I nodded politely to him. Took another bite.

He stalked up and looked me up and down. "I don't know you."

I swallowed. *Be cool. You can carry this off.* "Just passing through."

"East Coast by your accent. And your color's off. You're nothing but a halfer. Bet you've never seen the Demon."

"I've been to a dance." *Shit, they did call it a dance, didn't they? And something about a great demon?* "I've seen the Great Demon. I'm just here to earn some money. I'll be gone soon enough."

"Oh? Is Dominic trying to pick up territory out here? Tell him to go bugger himself."

I nodded. "Not that he'd listen to me . . . we have our differences."

Damn it, how do I get information out of him? What the hell did those killers say?

"All the stupid history he spouts." I looked the Hunter up and down. "But then I suppose you believe all the crap about the four brothers and such."

"It's not crap! How dare you defile the legends of our people."

I sighed. Loudly. "Yeah, go ahead. Convince me. Tell me your version." Took a big bite of burger.

Glare. "Sashoddifail entered the World in the fire of an undersea volcano . . . are you quite certain you've seen the All-Mother?"

I remembered the fire at the dancing ground . . . shifted nervously. *It was just smoke.*

The Hunter snickered. "Yeah, you've seen her. I'll bet you ran away like a yelping puppy." He laughed.

I probably blushed. Or possibly looked terrified.

He sat across the table from me and stared into my eyes. "She absorbed the essences of the life around her, and assumed the shape of the most advanced, the octopus."

I glowered. "Whales, dolphins, seals . . . "

"Shut up. The All-Mother preferred the shape of the octopus, the ability to grasp and make. She partook of all as she explored. And at the end of the water, there were more things. Bears, wolves, cougars . . . and man. And in man she found the perfect mix. Intelligence and hands." The Hunter wiggled his fingers in the air.

Like he's telling a story to a little kid. But I'm not going to interrupt his insanity.

"And Man lived with Dogs. The All-Mother partook of both, and understood that they were two species living together, not just one. That together they were greater than both separately. And so when she created us, she made the four sons both dog and man, as mutable as she herself."

I wiggled my own fingers. "With cat's claws. A tall tale for the kiddies. I figure the four sons were escapees from a government lab."

The Hunter growled as he stood and loomed. "Don't go spouting that heresy around us, Puppy. We've danced with the Demon and we know the truth. I think you'd better head back East where you belong." He stalked out.

I sat and stared at what was left of my dinner. Appetite gone.

My version makes more sense.

It was just smoke.

Chapter Fourteen

Back to the job hunt

"Bloody stupid animals. Why do people have pets, anyway? Why should I care about a stray dog?" Rachel flipped pancakes onto plates, added bacon, and served her sister and brother-in-law.

"We can check the pound. Not that he's ours, but . . . we could claim him." Nicole was at least trying to look sympathetic.

Kris just looked thoughtful, and said nothing.

Rachel stomped back to the kitchen and poured more batter on the griddle. "I'm going to go drop off some more resumes."

"And drive around looking for a big brown dog," Nicole called back. "Umm, good pancakes."

"It's all in how you stir the mix." Rachel flipped this batch. "Anyone going to want more? No? Ha! All mine!" She piled them up and carried the plate out to the table.

"No bacon?" Nicole looked at her last half strip

guiltily.

"I ate mine while I was cooking. Now for dessert. Gobs of melted butter and real maple syrup. It doesn't get any better than this."

Kris grinned and shook his head. "I give you two five years max before you're both on diets and trying to resist pancakes."

"Never!" Rachel dug into her pancakes. Swallowed the first bite. "Although I do need to start running regularly again."

"Mmm." Nicole swallowed.

"Today, I'm going to job hunt locally. Monday . . . unless I get some interest around here, I'll start downtown. Ugh. I hate long commutes." She wolfed down the pancakes and dashed for the shower.

I'll cover the other end of the strip center. Then up and over a couple of blocks, see if anyone needs a receptionist. Might as well start with Handyman Central.

She parked and walked in.

Not really dressed for this particular job, but . . .

And there was a computer thing right there inside the door, to use to apply for a job.

68

Well, that's handy.

She filled everything out and pushed the send button. And headed back out to check out the other stores, drop off three resumes, then head for the little clump of medical places.

Dentists, orthodontists, physical therapy, 24 hour Urgent Care . . . Every single one asked about training in medical billing and coding . . .

Her phone buzzed. "Hello?"

"Hi. Is this Rachel Ball?"

"Yes, how may I help you?"

"I'm Nina Harris, assistant manager at Handyman Central. Your resume says you've had accounting classes . . . we're looking for an online and phone billing clerk . . . Could you come in this afternoon for an interview?"

"Absolutely. I can be there at three, if that works for you?"

"It does. See you at three."

Rachel clicked off before letting out a whoop. "An interview! Yay! Even if it doesn't work, it's a great start." She hustled home for a quick freshen up and slight wardrobe adjustment.

More practical, less ritzy than a big business receptionist would wear. But still dressed for business.

She asked at customer service, and was directed to the back of the store.

Miss Nina Harris was brisk and businesslike with sharp eyes under neat short gray hair.

No HR nonsense here.

And even better, they were desperate for someone who knew spreadsheets and could actually communicate with people over the phone. Take orders, calculate taxes, or remember to get tax exempt ID. She appeared to be an exemplary boss, especially when she offered Rachel a job on the spot.

Rachel accepted, filled out her own forms, then started right in on the backlog of orders. She worked late and bounced home happy and ravenous.

Kris grinned and shook his head. "Give it a month. Bet it'll be driving you up the wall."

"Kris!" Nicole was half scolding and half laughing. "Here. I saved your dinner."

"Woof?"

They exchanged glances and Rachel stomped around to the sliding glass doors. Stone smiled through the glass.

"Don't you dare use that charm on me, buster! I *worried* about you." She slid the door and let him in. "Do that again and I'll haul you down to the vet to get your wanderlust surgically removed!"

"Woof!"

Nicole burst out laughing. "That was definitely a reproving and indignant woof."

Rachel sniff. "Bad dog. Just see if I share my dinner with you." And got the big eyed treatment.

Nicole rolled her eyes and brought him a bowl of mashed potatoes and gravy.

***

Her second day of work, she bounced from getting carts loaded to be picked up by the people who'd ordered things online, to more ordinary bookkeeping. Miss Nina made five trips to the bank, looking more cheerful each time.

"Girl, I don't know where you find the energy!"

Allison Higgins, at the next desk, gave her a dark look.

Rachel ignored it and grabbed three online orders for cabinets. "Be right back."

The only purple shirt in the department was her terrified Leo. She pulled the big flat up to him. "Hi Leo. I need three sink cabinets. All sixty inches. Three different styles."

He glanced at the ticket and flashed a smile. "Right this way. Fortunately I'll only have to climb for one of them." He stopped and slid one off the head-level shelf of the huge racks. "Does the barcode match?"

She checked. "Yep. And then an Old Colonial." They walked down rows of cabinets in every size and shape imaginable. This one was on the bottom shelf.

Then he fetched a rolling ladder, locked the wheels and climbed up to pull the third one.

He called out the number to be sure. A quick grin. "I don't want to have to haul it back up!"

The numbers matched, and he just slid it out, held it over his head and walked down the ladder like it was easy.

Men have all the muscles. No fair! Especially when they come with good balance and coordination. And this one's got it all plus good looking.

"Fantastic. I've got two more orders, if you'd like to look them over while I haul this load up front?"

"Sure." He glanced at the lists. "Right, two more big carts, coming up."

He had one cabinet loaded and was up on the ladder when she returned. She checked the number he called down, the one already on the cart . . .

Cute and competent. A nice smile.

"So . . . why'd you run off the other day?"

"I was afraid I'd be late when I'd just started here?" He looked at her hopefully.

She shook her head.

He heaved a sigh. "I spotted a relative of mine. My family is . . . there's a lot of problems. My one attempt to, oh, I don't know. Just be around them? Maybe even like them? Complete disaster. Guess I learned why I was raised far away from them, in Atlanta . . . so what's next on the list?"

"Regency Natural Oak. Five pieces."

"I'll get another cart." He strode off.

Leo. Atlanta. Surely he's not Leonard Stone? She bit her lip. I'm not going to ask. I'll . . . I'll find out if he deserves a good dog like Stone!

And he ran away from a guy who looked a heck of a lot like him. So either his family is horrid, or he's a coward. Or both, of course.

Chapter Fifteen

Sending a message

They let me sleep inside, closed in the laundry room. So I didn't have any excuses for not . . . somehow doing something about the Hunters of Men. I opened the laundry room's inside door as quietly as I possibly could, and paced down the hallway. The good thing about retractable claws was not worrying about clicking on the hardwood floor.

Up the stairs to the computer room. Nice and quiet. I closed the door behind me and checked carefully that Nicole's speakers were turned off. Then I turned her machine on and worried about the best way—secure and requiring the least amount of two-claw-typing—way to spoof a sender's location. I'd been pretty good a few years ago. Badly out of practice but I'd give it a try.

Thank you for saving all your passwords!

The computer took no skill at all . . . A quick internet search . . . who did I want to send this to, anyway? Arizona and New Mexico were both involved . . . Right, FBI. I got their email address and then got to work laying a false trail, a misleading backtrace, and then typed a very brief message. A rough location for the warehouse in Albuquerque I'd been taken to, and the addresses of the three houses here. "The werewolves live here."

Retractable claws were not made for typing . . . and if they didn't understand that there really were werewolves, then I wasn't sending the locations to the right place, anyway. I hit the send button and erased my tracks.

I stared at the computer . . . then turned it off.

There's no one I want to talk to.

I crept back to the laundry room and slept.

Chapter Sixteen

The first big break

"The two bodies in New Mexico have turned out to be members of the Forty-eight gang. The Albuquerque Field Office incident crew is taking over the scene, and has expanded the search area.

"Besides the two human bodies, we've found the remains of two large dogs. Much chewed by critters, but with a time of death very close to that of the human victims. The map of the area . . . This is a cattle ranch—four thousand acres of rugged sparse grazing, rarely visited—a hundred and ten miles west of Albuquerque and eight miles north of Interstate Forty. They've got trained cadaver dogs enroute to see if there are any of the sorts of hidden graves we've seen elsewhere."

A map of the state, then a close up with the marked locations of the parked car and the two human bodies. The canine remains were a quarter and a third of the way back to I40.

"We're getting daily updates."

Kris Kovac repressed a sigh. *If I was in DC, I'd probably have been sent out there as the lead investigator. Now I'll have to wait for someone else to write the report and circulate it.*

Dammit. However much nicer it is out here, otherwise. I feel like I'm in a backwater.

"We have a new detailed analysis of those extra chromosomes from the labs." Masterson clicked on the big screen and they watched the whole dog and pony show.

"Genetic engineering as the direct transfer of DNA from one organism to another was first accomplished by Herbert Boyer and Stanley Cohen in 1972. The first genetically modified animal was a mouse created in 1974 by Rudolf Jaenisch." The man on the screen shrugged. "So it's 2029. We've had fifty-five years, in theory, to do something disastrous to ourselves. In actuality, serious expertise has existed for less than half that, but it's clear from this Forty-eight Gang that it has been done."

A ferocious scowl. "Despite the century old kill sites. The genetic oddities *must* be much more recent."

Kris had seen presentations by the man before, met him in person once. Dr. Daniel Reid.

So the experts don't think it's a natural mutation. Something deliberate. But we're getting third generation DNA showing up.

"The two extra chromosomes are not natural. Not accidental duplications of other human chromosomes or even parts of them. They are hodgepodge collections of control genes from several species, mostly canine and feline, although we haven't pinned down the exact species. And there are some oddities that might be from an octopus, or . . . something else. Other labs have suggested genetic engineering of those chromosomes, but work of that nature has never been demonstrated. We have identified epigenetic switches on some of the odd genes that turn the genes on during adrenaline surges, then turn them back off.

"Of course, we're still studying them . . . what physical effect they could possibly have is hard to say. Faster reflexes? Stronger? Neither dogs nor cats are known for endurance, so possibly just in bursts?" Dr. Reid scowled at the camera. "It would be nice to have an actual individual to observe and test. The evidence indicates that they are completely fertile with ordinary people, so find me some children from outside the criminal gangs, eh?"

"Oh, how does that work, with the extras not interfering? Best guess is they're mostly non-functional. Next best guess is they don't turn on until triggered by something—such as puberty. Eh, we need an actual—better yet several—live persons."

"Now the two bodies in New Mexico."

He tapped at a computer and a new chart popped up. "And we know interbreeding with outsiders works because of these new results we've just started studying, from New Mexico. An all new, never seen before individual. Different Y chromosome, different Mitochondrial line. He has both of the extra chromosomes, and enough overlap with the other genes that the best match is great-grandson of both LA2 and SC7 with outside women who both had daughters, and the son of one of those daughters married, or whatever, the daughter of the other half forty-eight daughter, and produced this fellow."

Make that, fourth generation.

"His DNA was from the usual fake dog bites, and also from blood on ropes found at the site. This is, however, the first time we've gotten actual bodies of gang members to study. This outsider apparently killed two of the Southwest group."

Kris leaned forward. "But the spitting on fake dog bites motif points to someone very familiar with the gang. Not an outsider."

The video, of course, rattled on without pause. "Well, details of the autopsy . . . both the victims had odd skeletal abnormalities. Whether these are typical of the gang, an effect of the artificial chromosomes, more ordinary birth defects, or deliberate post-natal restrictions of growth is an interesting question."

What? Like the old Chinese foot wrapping? Or unset breaks?

"So, in any case, they've been identified as sons of KC5 and KC8, based on semen samples from the 2018 attack in Kern County California where at least ten men raped, killed, dismembered, cooked, and ate four women . . . "

The pictures bore a definite resemblance to the boys in New Orleans. Outthrust face, light brown hair.

More DNA pictures . . . "our reconstructions of the women in the gang, from the DNA their sons have been leaving around . . . "

Kris barely paid attention as the technical terms flew.

West of Albuquerque? North of I-40? What date? Rachel must have driven past within 48 hours of the killing. I wonder if her dash cam would show anything interesting? At least I don't have to actually worry that the dog she picked up is a werewolf.

.

.

.

Right?

He mentally kicked himself and switched his attention to the screen.

". . . And so in addition to the one hundred and seventeen identified male members of the gang, we are postulating twenty-five adult women adding to the gene pool. Status in the gang unknown, number of children unknown."

The doctor glared out of the vid screen. "I need more samples. Do I have to find and hire a hacker to get into genetic databases?"

And I need a description of those dead dogs . . . although it's hard to imagine Stone as trained to kill. And he has a tag, former elderly owners.

I'll start by tracking down that son of theirs. Leonard Stone. I need to do that anyway . . . and now it's quasi-pertinent to the case.

He typed out a request for pictures and DNA on the dogs . . . *they'll think I'm insane . . .* He added a request for breed identification, and if that breed or breeds required DNA testing, to check any matches, or even partial matches that might be useful in tracking down the owners . . .

And dash cams. He'd check and see if Rachel even had one. And then . . . what? An open call for dash cam footage right then would alert the Forty-eights. And unless he could find someone who had downloaded the right times, the small memory capacity of most dash cams would have been over-written already.

When Masterson asked for additional input or suggestions, Kris brought up the dash cam potential. "Maybe quietly ask truckers? See if any of them regularly download and save trips. And those dogs . . . I'd like a DNA test . . . for breed or breeds, so we can . . . so the Albuquerque office can check breeders in the area."

Masterson paused. "I know the costs of the test

have dropped . . . "

"Sir, this is the first big break we've had on the Forty Eights. We need to check *everything*."

"How true—and the pictures from New Orleans barely constituted a break, at that."

The meeting finally broke up and Kris went home and checked—Stone was gone again—and Rachel's car did indeed have a dash cam. He pulled the chip and copied it to his computer, then headed back to the office.

She hadn't driven much since her arrival. That part of her drive was still there. Kris trawled slowly through the trip, from just outside Albuquerque. He noted license plates. *Crimes are often solved by trudging along looking at everything.*

He spotted the big dog limping along the road. Away from the scene of the slaughter.

I need a picture of the dead dogs at the scene.

That evening, he listened to Rachel's newest plans to corral her dog.

I should haul him down to HQ. Or something. At least get him away from my family, in case he really has been trained to attack and kill people. But that's stupid. There's human saliva in the bites. Fake dog

84

bites, not real. The Albuquerque scene was probably the Forty-eights versus a drug smuggling gang.

"Don't bother getting too elaborate. He's not your dog yet."

Rachel glowered. "He could get hit by a car."

"Any dog that can open and close doors and gates is probably pretty street-wise." Kris winced.

This is stupid. I do not have a werewolf member of the Forty-eights sleeping on my back porch!

Chapter Seventeen

Weekend Crunch

Saturday was supposed to be the busiest day of the week for the store, so Rachel dressed, packed a lunch . . . gave into the impulse to make a second sandwich . . . just in case . . . some random cute guy was hungry.

But it turned into a day of completely different kind of busy from the weekdays. Millions of shoppers, but no contractors. Millions of small sales. Lots of medium sales. Only two tickets for the warehouse. She spotted Leo three times, helping customers with items on high shelves.

And being scolded by "Miss Nina" as everyone called her boss.

Miss Nina looked over at Rachel. "And you haven't taken your lunch either, have you? Go! both of you. You have to last all day, you know!"

Rachel fetched her cooler, which was still cool

inside, and looked at Leo who was contemplating the selections in a vending machine. "Rot your teeth eating like that."

He snickered. "What! I can't live on fast food?"

She looked at the packet of cupcakes in his hand. "That doesn't even rise to the status of fast food. Not that I don't love those things . . . " She looked back at her cooler.

Well? Have I got the nerve?

"Trade you one of my sandwiches for a cupcake."

He grinned.

Ohmygawd he's fantastic when he grins. I swear his eyes twinkled.

She pulled out both sandwiches and grinned back. "I made two, in case I stayed late."

"And with that madhouse out there . . . "

"We'll be staying late. But I forgot how late my official lunch is." She pushed a sandwich across the old scarred table.

He opened his packet, and pulled out a cupcake. He handed the packet with the other cupcake across the table. Took a bite out of his own, and started opening the sandwich bag.

Rachel snickered.

"Don't worry, no chance I won't eat it all."

Rachel grinned. "I can hear my mother's voice in my head."

Leo grinned back and managed a falsetto. "Not until after dinner, young lady."

Oh dear . . . all crinkle eyes and dimples . . . happy.

"Exactly. And what would your mother have said? 'Don't spoil your dinner, dear?' No?"

"More like 'I swear you're going to eat me out of house and home, you bottomless teenage black hole!' and then she'd laugh." He looked wistful, shrugged. Popped the last of the cupcake into his mouth.

"Do you talk to them often?"

He shook his head. "They're both dead, now. Just . . . old age. They were my foster parents, the only parents I remember. The state thought they were too old to adopt me . . . but they raised me from the time I was about five through a year of college."

"But you know your extended family?"

"After Mom died—about a month after Dad—I decided to track them down. What a mistake. I was better off with dreams." Took a bite of ham sandwich. "Umm, this is good."

Rachel nodded. "My parents sold the house, bought a condo on a golf course and didn't *quite* kick me out, but they made it clear that it was time for me to fly the nest. They phone every week. Generally to complain that we never visit."

Leo raised his eyebrows.

"Which we do! But we're busy. My sister's husband transferred down here—he's from Tucson and he missed the desert—and they're trying to have a baby so she hasn't been working. When the company I was working for folded, I decided to come check out the job prospects here." She paused for a bite.

"I noticed your car had Tennessee plates."

She nodded, swallowed. "Nashville. Phoenix is going to take a while to feel like home."

He nodded. "I guess I've been in the desert for . . . three weeks? It's really different. Even though I think pristine green lawns are unnatural, I'm so used to them that all these cactus and rock yards look scraggly and uncared for."

Rachel nodded. "And the crab grass is the worst. I mean, I know it'll come back when it gets rain, but right now? It's just brown!"

She stayed late, not going home until the doors were locked, the last receipts in and counted. Leo stayed for restocking and a final sweep, and left a bit before she finally staggered out to her car and drove the short distance home.

Sunday the store opened late, so she slept in, got in a probably-not-actually-two-miles run, with Stone who'd actually been there, for a change. Ate breakfast, fed the dog—who promptly disappeared—and headed back to work. It wasn't nearly as busy as Saturday, but still impressive. Contractor orders for cabinets were coming in, so she got to admire Leo's strength and balance again.

Chapter Eighteen

Research

I got to work early, and instead of a lunch hour, I took two and found the local library. They didn't have anything I hadn't already read on werewolves, but there were some on 'Skinwalkers' . . . that I put away hastily.

Almost scarier than my family!

And books on magic . . . stage, nope, Tarot cards? Umm, don't think so. Oooo, demonology for beginners . . . maybe I could find out where the hunters got their delusions from. Natural Magic? I really didn't think I could do anything "magic" but I suppose, I mean . . . I certainly wasn't ordinary . . . supernatural seemed a bit of a stretch, though.

A bit to my surprise, an out-of-state driver's license and a local address—I gave them the store's—was good enough for the library card. I trotted back to the store, put the books in my otherwise empty locker and got back to work.

And after, I headed straight home, books, and then clothes, in a bag.

I got scolded for having escaped, and locked in the laundry room while they went out for dinner.

Yay! As soon as they were out of the house, I streaked for my clothes stash and dragged them all inside. It took two trips in dog-form, but I needed to wash *everything*.

Only a small spill trying to pour the laundry detergent. I'm more dexterous than a real dog, but that's more because of being able to think how to do things with paws, than my paws being not-quite standard dog or cat paws.

Anyhow, I got the wash started. And stretched out on the living room rug to read about demonology. Brrr. If the author wasn't a believer, he was sure good at pretending.

The sound of the garage door opening caught me by surprise.

I shoved the books under the couch and ran for the laundry room. Jumped up and stopped the washing machine, closed the inner door . . .

"Oh! Look who's a good dog! You stayed in the . . . " Rachel voice trailed off.

I sat there looking innocent as she stepped past me and shoved the outside door closed.

Oops, left it ajar.

Click.

And unlocked.

"Honestly Stone! I didn't know dogs could do things like that! I don't know what to try next. C'mon out."

Oh well, at least she didn't notice the washing machine stopped in mid-rinse cycle.

Nicole had kicked off her shoes, and rubbed her feet. "Why do I wear things like these monstrosities?" She leaned to scoop them up and headed for the master bedroom, downstairs, opposite the garage and laundry room . . .

The TV clicked on to an advertisement. Kris put the remote down and followed her.

Rachel headed upstairs.

Yes!

I hustled into the laundry room and clicked the resume button. Closed the door behind me. With the sound of the news on the TV, maybe I could get everything washed. The dryer . . . umm, this was going to take both luck and cunning.

I trotted back to the living room and flopped down where I'd be in the way of anyone heading for the laundry room.

And watched the news. About the discovery of two bodies in the desert, on the New Mexico side of the state line. Apparently killed by an animal, but the coroner would have more to say after the autopsy. The police suspected a falling out between drug runners.

Two bodies.

I'd killed both of them. I wasn't going to feel bad about fighting for my life. I wasn't.

But . . . Oh, dammit all, why hadn't I doubled back and taken my wallet away with me?

I heard the faint whirr of the spin cycle spinning down and eased back down the hallway. With a noisy advertisement for cover I got into the laundry room and closed the door behind me.

And had my first set back. I couldn't reach down into the washing machine and grab stuff.

I cursed mentally and reached mentally for the human-form that lurked in the depths of my bones and my mind.

Ouch, ouch, ouch!

My arms elongated, front toes extended . . . I

96

grabbed clothes and stuffed them into the dryer as quickly as I could, while the change was still under way.

Quick check, got them all!

"Stone? Are you back here letting yourself out?"

Oh, oh, oh! Bad timing!

I reached for the dog-form as I quietly closed the dryer door.

The doorknob turned.

I leaped and leaned on the interior door, as pain wracked bones that suddenly didn't know which way to morph.

"Woof!" I turned off the light. Maybe she wouldn't notice . . . problems . . . in the dark . . .

"Silly dog! I can't let you out if you don't get out of the way."

She shoved.

I braced myself, hands against the door, and held the door closed.

Reached for the dog-inside.

Be a dog. C'mon body, go back to being a dog.

Okay. My hands were looking pretty dog-like. I rubbed one on my nose. Nope, still a human nose.

Paw back on the door as Rachel put some muscle

into it.

"Dog!"

Another quick feel. Ears, the ears were good.

"Woof!" I tried to sound happy, not frantic and in pain. What I really wanted to do was howl in pain and frustration.

Deep breathing, relax. C'mon, you learned how to control your form that interesting summer before high school.

I rubbed my . . . muzzle, wagged my tail . . . a couple of more deep breaths and I backed off as the door opened.

Rachel peeked around the door. "Good Grief! Get down, you silly mutt."

I backed up and dropped down to all fours.

"Woof!'

"Good. Grief. You are the weirdest dog! C'mon."

I followed her to the living room and flopped on the rug. Tried to relax, tried to will away the aches and pain.

Whew! Next time I'll have to find a laundromat. This was just too harrowing.

And I still need to turn on the dryer.

They'd run out of news and started chatting about the weather—about how dry it had been and hopefully they wouldn't have something called a haboob.

I hadn't a clue what they were talking about, so I put my head back down. The ache was wearing off . . . I'd never tried to switch back in mid-change before. And while it was useful to know it worked, I really hoped I'd never have to do it again!

And then . . . football! Yes! Monday Night Football!

I couldn't help it, my tail wagged madly. Seahawks versus the Cardinals.

Rachel reached down and scratched that itchy spot between my shoulder blades. "So, you like football too, Stone?"

"Woof!"

I even stood for the National Anthem.

And with the crowd cheering a long runback, I slipped into the laundry room and turned on the dryer.

Closed the door and slipped back just as Rachel noticed I was gone. I gave her a hopeful look and tail wag and headed for the kitchen. Sat and stared at the refrigerator.

"Oh, Dog, really!" Rachel had followed me, shaking her head.

"Give him a hotdog." Nicole called over the roar of the crowd.

Rachel pulled out a pack with only two hotdogs left. She pulled one out and offered it to me.

I gave her my best shocked look and turned to stare at the microwave.

She started laughing. "Oh? You want it hot? How about a bun and mustard."

"Woof!" I danced happily around, and was rewarded with a proper hotdog.

Then we watched more football.

The buzz of the dryer came with the first touchdown, and I bolted down the hall to stop it before it buzzed again. I opened the back door, dropped the dryer door and scooped everything out to the back porch. I had to make three trips, being in dog form, to get everything around the corner to my hideout, then I closed the dryer, the back door, the inside door, and flopped down to watch the rest of the game.

That was a much needed task, all wrapped up.

All is well with the world.

Chapter Nineteen

So what's scariest?

Rachel spotted the dog leaving from the corner of her eye.

What is he up to now? He keeps going back to the laundry room, which is really odd. And pretty funny. How on Earth did someone train him to close doors?

She got up and walked down the hall . . . eased the door open . . . Oops, the pup had left the back door open—probably because the dryer door was in the way.

Don't tell me Stone opens cupboards and stuff . . . and why is the dryer warm?

She peered at the pile of clothes outside the door . . . men's clothes? A purple shirt . . . just like the Handyman Central shirts . . .

She reached and turned over the purple shirt.

The embroidered name was clear.

Leo

She backed away . . . slipped out the inner door

and walked back to the living room.

Stared blankly at the screen.

Stone's a werewolf.

Dog. Whatever.

She shook her head.

Oh don't be stupid.

Did Stone find his owner Leo and lead him back here? And finding us gone, Leo decided to do his laundry while we were gone? That's creepy enough. And it would explain why Stone keeps going back there.

Oh God. Is Leo a rapist? Is he stalking me? Doing creepy things before he strikes?

All things considered, I think I'd prefer a were-dog to a creepy stalker.

She froze at a thump. Looked down at the big dog stretching out, looking tired.

Of course, a werewolf would explain all the locks and doors and gates. And he has to run off to work every day. And likes his hotdogs hot, in buns, with mustard.

Why does he work . . . well, duh, for money. This isn't a stupid movie where he's the filthy rich head of a pack of werewolves.

Not that I believe in werewolves. But . . .

I wonder when the full moon is?

And why was he limping down the highway?

After the game, she gave Stone a bowl of kibble and filled a bowl with water—out on the back patio. And made sure the outside laundry room door was both locked and a broom "just happened" to fall where it barricaded the door.

Not that someone couldn't get in . . . but they'd make a lot of noise, and Rachel was quite certain that FBI Agents carried loaded guns. *Kris probably sleeps with one under his pillow.*

Maybe I need one.

***

And yet, the next morning she kind of missed the big mutt, who had departed sometime during the night.

Except . . . he'll be at work, won't he?

Slapped her forehead.

Rachel, listen to yourself. Leo is not a werewolf. Maybe he's creepy, or maybe he's homeless. Whichever, you'd better stay away from him.

Chapter Twenty

Magic

Rachel's sister was the only one home when I got there. I hid my clothes, and trotted around to the back door.

"Woof!" I sat and put on my best smile and wagged my tail when she let me in.

"Honestly, dog. If you weren't so charming, you'd be in big trouble." She scooped dry dog food, refilled my water bowl, and left me staring at the kibble.

Drat.

But I still ate every bit of it.

I checked that Nicole was upstairs in what they called the computer room and reached under the couch to retrieve my library books. Demonology had been a bit much, so I tried the Natural Magic book. It started out like the Power of Positive Thinking, meditating and visualizing the results you wanted, and then visualizing all the steps to get there. I think she left out the bit about "and then get off your ass and do it," but it wasn't what I'd call magic.

I ought to have quit there, but the author dived into crystals, aroma therapy, and feng shui. It was interesting in a sort of "Please tell me no one actually believes that" way.

I shoved the books back under the couch when I heard Nicole coming down the stairs. Wagged my tail and concentrated on how lovely a ham sandwich would be. Fresh bread, a touch of mayo and mustard, thin sliced swiss cheese, that delicious smoked ham I could smell from here . . .

She walked into the kitchen and fixed a beautiful big ham sandwich. And sat down and ate it.

Clearly I was going to have to work harder on my visualization.

I stared at her. *Poor dog. Needs a bite of ham.*

She cleared everything away and walked out, patted me on the head. "Poor dog. Do you need a bite of ham?"

She walked back to the fridge and got me one.

Definitely going to practice visualizations.

Chapter Twenty-one

Leonard Stone

Kris drummed his fingers nervously on his desk.

It had been a nice relaxed weekend—the sister-in-law working and her wretched dog had disappeared again—so he had the house and Nicole to himself most of the time.

But Monday had brought a new problem.

He ran through the report again.

Leonard Stone was an orphaned or abandoned child. The case files were brief. A naked boy of about five years of age, found wandering the streets. Didn't speak. No physical cause. Neglect suspected. Stuck in a foster home while a search for his parents was carried out. Unsuccessfully. The elderly foster parents had been working on his speech, kept the boy, raised him . . .

The boy's high school yearbook was online. The pictures were quite clear. Outthrust face, broad, heavy jaw with a long chin. Grinning out of a studio portrait, accepting an award, beaming elderly couple behind him. Winning a track event. Wrestling team. Football team.

"At least his hair is darker." Kris rubbed his face.

Dark brown, about the color of the dog's hair. Have I got AQ1 living in my house? Maybe I should go home and shoot him.

Except . . . what happened out on that cattle ranch? Did he kill two fellow gang members?

Shit. If I'm going to believe in werewolves, four gang members died out there. Were killed. Why?

I should hear soon about the DNA test on those dead dogs.

His eyes slid to the pictures of the messy half eaten remains. Big heavy short haired dogs. Pale brindle hair. Smallish ears mostly erect, just the tips flopped.

Damn it all. They probably looked a lot like Stone before they got all chewed up.

Leonard Stone had received one traffic ticket in Vermont two years ago, one in Maine, just six months ago.

So what was he doing out on a cattle ranch west of Albuquerque?

Or limping down an Arizona highway.

Looking like a dog.

He checked his email. His requested DNA analysis of the dogs still hadn't arrived. But the raw crime scene description of the Albuquerque site came in just before noon.

He sat back and studied it. Nodded to his boss as Brent Masterson stuck his head in the door.

Masterson eyed the chart on Kris' computer.

"How's it compare to our sites, or the Carolina sites, for that matter?"

"In the Carolina's they buried everything except the poles. Here they dumped the bodies—or what was left of them—down old abandoned mines and caved them in. Well, you've read all of those reports."

Masterson nodded.

"But in New Mexico they didn't survive to hide it. It's nice to see one of their killing grounds that hasn't been concealed. Nice and clear. A single stake, rather than the usual three or four. But the hole was freshly dug, not a long standing . . . installation, so to speak. The post was close to the north side of a circle cleared of vegetation. A fire on the south side of the clearing. Their victim was tied with ropes, that's the way they usually do it, from the marks on the victims. But here we have the intact ropes, knots still tied. He must have wiggled loose."

"This is only their third male victim, right?"

"Right, and the only one, male or female, related to them. A traitor?"

"Sure sounds like it." Brent tapped a spot on the map.

"Clothing. The victim's, we believe." Kris scrolled through the report looking . . . "Sorry, I just got this and I haven't gotten to any names . . . Oh, they have three IDs from the site. From both of the bodies, and a wallet in the clothing there by the stake." Kris scrolled down . . .

Body #1
Neil Sampson Wolfe
654 Wanderlust Dr #132
Albuquerque, NM

Body #2
Kenneth F. Wolfe
654 Wanderlust Dr #65
Albuquerque, NM

ID in clothing

    Leonard S. Stone

    6931 Green Meadow Ln

    Bangor, ME

Masterson stuck his finger on the last. "An outsider. A feud within the Forty-eights?"

Kris swallowed, trying to regain his composure. "We, umm . . . The four groups are quite distinct, not much mixing. So gang warfare is certainly a possibility."

"We need to find Leonard Stone."

Kris shivered. *So the dog's owner was in the area, with the dog. The dog survived . . . so where is the man?*

He scrolled further . . . the two Albuquerque addresses . . . the apartment complex manager had been puzzled by the abrupt departure of six tenants. All six apartments were stripped and very clean. They were being swabbed for DNA.

"Damn. They must have found out before the killing site was discovered." Kris bit his lip. *Better early than late.* "As it happens, I was looking for a

Leonard Stone prior to this, on what I thought was a private matter."

"Oh?"

"Yes. My sister-in-law's come to stay with us. She took I40 all the way from Nashville to Flagstaff, passing the kill site about 48 hours after the killing. Roughly thirty miles into Arizona she picked up a big dog limping down the road, heading west. We traced the tags to a Harriet Stone in Atlanta, Georgia. The vet's office said both the Stones had died five years ago, and perhaps the dog was with their son—they thought his name was Leonard."

Kris stared at the screen. "I think I'll see about getting a bite impression, just to double check that there really isn't a dog involved in the actual killings."

"Indeed." Masterson nodded. "If we can locate Stone, perhaps we can get close enough—returning his lost dog—to actually get our hands on him."

Kris nodded. "Maybe an ad? A 'Found Dog' sort of thing?"

"Let me coordinate with Albuquerque first."
And maybe I should coordinate at home.
Stone is definitely sleeping on the porch.
With all the doors locked.

"Right." Kris took a deep breath. "And it looks like we'd better start looking around Atlanta, for kill sites. And find out what happened to the Stones."

***

Kris was halfway home when his boss called.

"Some DOD Agency, complete with armored personnel carriers, has descended on Albuquerque. The State Police, County Sheriff, and our field office are all off the Forty-eight kill site."

Kris sighed. "I suspect we're next on their agenda, and we won't make the 'need-to-know' list. Dammit. I wonder what triggered this?"

"I figure they're going to have to go public with all these old mass graves being connected, the work of a single gang."

"Oh." Kris nodded. "And they want to look like they're serious about it. That's . . . what the hell are they going to do with an APC? Do they have a lead on what and where to raid? Dammit, I want in on this."

And what about the bloody dog?

I don't believe in werewolves, vampires or zombies.

But I haven't gotten anything back on the dog

DNA . . . Surely that couldn't be what triggered a . . . response from the DOD?

The dog showed up to watch Monday Night Football, wagging his tail whenever the Raiders scored.

***

And as he'd half expected, the DOD arrived early Tuesday morning.

"Brian Wright. Pleased to meet you. I need all of your information on the Forty-eights."

"Right. Umm, which branch of the DOD are you with?"

"You don't need to know that."

"I . . . see. Have you got the preliminary report on the kill site discovered last week? Good. It's six years old. What I'm looking at right now is more likely relevant to the New Mexico site." Kris winced internally and pulled up the file on Leonard Stone. "The strong resemblance to the teenagers in New Orleans leads me to believe he's related, but by the history we have on him, he may not be part of the gang. I was wondering, in fact, if he might be AQ1. I have not yet queried Atlanta as to whether they have DNA of the lost child later named Leonard Stone."

Wright leaned over and studied Stone's pictures. "Now that is interesting. We need to find this young man . . . why were you looking for him?"

"Tracing a lost dog."

The DOD agent straightened abruptly.

Kris leaned back and studied the man. "I requested a DNA analysis of the dog remains, for breed identification, maybe find the breeder, check his sales records. I haven't heard back at all. Do you have that information.?"

"That is need-to-know only. Where's the dog now?"

"Over the fence and gone. So . . . what are the dogs?"

The man's eyes narrowed. "That is no longer any of your business." A brief drumming of fingernails. "And you didn't send an anonymous email about . . . anything. Did you?"

"What?"

He waved it away. "Someone was cute and tried to hide their tracks."

"Through my account?" Kris eyed him. Got a nod.

"Home or here?"

"Home."

"Right. And you're not going to tell me anything about it, are you?"

A thin smile.

Kris grabbed a thumb drive, downloaded all of his files on everything to do with the Forty-eights and Leonard Stone and handed it over.

Wright glowered.

Kris shrugged and deleted them from his computer.

Wright nodded and produced a card. "Send me anything else as quickly as you can." And walked out.

Kris looked back at his computer. *Stupid. Surely he knows I've got back ups. Most likely he's got me tapped and is waiting to see what I do. So we've got a script kiddie playing with . . . dammit. Stone is not a werewolf and he didn't send an email from my home.*

And Mr. Wright?

God only knows what, or even how many little subagencies the DOD has swallowed up over the years. Weird stuff . . . yeah. I shouldn't be surprised they've got a weird stuff division.

He thought about Wright.

And I'm not going to speculate about a joke of an agency that has to investigate reports of werewolves. Nor will I speculate about it being where people get shuffled when they can't be fired, but aren't wanted elsewhere. Merely because he's throwing around need-to-know like he's showing off.

I am going to leave the Forty-eights in the hopefully competent hands of the DOD, and get back to what I ought to be doing.

Which, now that I think of it, is get back to work on the matter of embezzlement on the reservation . . . I'll check if Rick's got anything new . . . talk to the Boss . . . think about home security.

Or what to do if the dog shows up tonight.

Because if the dogs were just Mastiffs or some such, why not just say so?

***

Kris left work on time for a change.

Was met at the door with an ardent kiss from Nicole.

"So now you're being left alone all day by both your husband and your sister?"

"Umm, and the dog. I suspect he was off before

you were this morning. Or maybe last night. I feel responsible for him, which is silly. Not my dog, you know?"

"Yes . . . I noticed an absence of dog, this morning. We'll just have to see if he comes back when he gets hungry."

And then we'll find out if Wright is watching me.

It was nice to have some time alone with Nicole.

Rachel bounced in just after eight, checked the backyard, shook her head. "Just as well. Bit of a nuisance, bound to be an issue with the neighbors."

Kris ignored her frequent glances toward the sliding glass door, and the unhappy downturn of her mouth.

Yeah, he's a good dog . . . sort of.

Chapter Twenty-two

A hike in the desert

Tuesdays and Wednesdays were my two off days every week. I bought a bunch of jerky and nuts at a store on the way home from work Monday, and ate kibble for breakfast.

Then I hopped a bus for Sun City.

And for lack of a better idea, I hiked further out Highway 60. Just because I'd tracked some Hunters headed this direction didn't mean they hadn't turned off somewhere. Or weren't coming out here regularly. Or ever again.

And yet, if they wanted solitude for summoning their Demon, the desert had plenty of places for them to be unobserved. But how far out would they go?

Where would they turn off the highway? North or south?

I stopped at a gas station and bought a cold soda . . . and spotted a rack of free touristy handouts. I sat in the shade and read them.

There was a big regional park to the south, outside Highway 303, which was probably that overpass right there. With hiking trails and so forth. Too many people or a target rich environment?

There was a canal running roughly north-south down toward it that looked a lot more hiker and dog friendly than walking along the highway, so I headed for it.

There was a big subdivision on the east side of the canal, with a high fence and no shelter for a wandering dog. The west side looked like it just backed up onto desert. So I hiked a bit further along Highway 60 and over the canal. Then I had to hop a barbed wire fence, but no big deal.

Two miles south, I found a taller than average bush and kicked back in a bit of shade. Chewed jerky.

Next time, maybe salami, cheese, and bread?

I closed my eyes. And just sort of *felt* everything around. The subdivision across the canal, people zipping around in cars. Pretty quiet in the middle of the day. If I was reading the map scale right, I should be able to feel the Hunters when they approached the intersection of 60 and 303.

And change . . . no, I'd change in a little bit. Be

ready . . . again assuming they'd be headed this way in the evening.

But the dance was as the sun set . . .

I shivered, despite the heat of the day.

I sat and meditated.

Stretched and yawned. Opened a bottle of obscenely expensive water, chewed more jerky. Meditated. Watched the rush hour hit, cars everywhere.

And something . . . them? Getting closer at any rate.

I dodged into the thicker brush, undressing, changing. Hiding my clothes. A pause to "look."

Sick green auras, two miles away, moving to my left. Turning away from me. They'd left the highway, and were heading *north*.

I ran northeast. Two miles to the highway. Where I managed to not get hit by any cars crossing it. Half a mile to a road, yes this was the road they were on. I followed it past a ritzy entrance to some upscale subdivision. I kept running as the Hunters increased their lead and pulled away, finally out of range of my perception.

Drat.

But I trotted along and followed the road to where it curved west . . .

There was a smaller lane going on straight . . . I checked it out but found nothing even though I circled out until nearly dawn.

There were no white glows in the cars. There was no brutal sacrifice last night!

So far as I can tell.

I panicked and ran back to my clothes and changed. Back over the fence and hustled into Sun City, took a bus down one stop past where I'd gotten on yesterday and hiked to the Kovac's. Rachel's car was parked in the street. Two brighter-than-most auras from inside.

I climbed their side fence and flopped on the ground to catch my breath. Then I changed and curled up to sleep until Rachel called me in the morning.

Wednesday. She had to work, I didn't. I snuck out for a breakfast burrito at the nearest fast food place, then home and flopped on the rug to nap.

Kris and Rachel had both left work. Nicole shook her head at me. "Tough day chasing cats Stone?"

"Woof!" *Lions and Tigers and Bears, according*

to the Hunter I'd had that interesting chat with. And Octopi. Eww!

"I'm going to go grocery shopping. Are you going to be here when I get back?"

"Woof." I was totally pooped, and even going back to the library sounded like too much work.

I need to run with Rachel in the morning. Just in case I wind up running all over the desert on a regular basis . . . Which I'll probably be doing at least once a week until I find out where they are going.

Chapter Twenty-three

Wrong ogles

It was kind of strange, not seeing Leo at work.

And the dog disappeared right after breakfast.

Which is good, because Nicole isn't home alone all day with a werewolf. But what does a werewolf do on his day off? Okay, he's not at the laundromat.

After all, he's got clean clothes for the week . . .

She stifled hysterical laughter at the thought, and told herself to start paying attention to other things around her.

But why does the dog disappear every morning and come back at night?

To watch football?

She grabbed a sheaf of web orders and marched determinedly off to start filling them.

Her only problem was getting a lot of ogles from the men who worked there, enough to make her skin crawl a bit. And that was before George got fresh . . . and rude when she said no.

Wednesday morning, Stone was grinning at the sliding glass doors, looking for breakfast.

She eyed him, shook her head. "Anyone want to bet he'll find a way to get out within the hour?"

No takers.

But when she got home, there was the dog, reading the newspaper he'd spread out on the living room floor.

Nicole laughed. "Doesn't that look funny?"

Yeah. REAL funny.

She popped upstairs to change and the papers were gone by the time she came back down. She didn't ask. It was safer to just assume Nicole had been the one to tidy up.

And of course the dog was gone Thursday morning, and Leo was at work, polishing off donuts and brushing crumbs off his nice clean shirt.

She grabbed web orders and looked around for a cart. She ignored George as he started forward, grinning, to "help" her.

And there was Leo towing a cart. "Here you go." And all day long jumping in to fetch things from the warehouse for her with a cheerful smile, as if he liked to climb ladders and manhandle heavy boxes.

Damn it, why is the werewolf the nice guy?

The store was having a Three-Day-Sale so Friday, Saturday, and Sunday turned into a non-stop madhouse.

She spotted Leo several times, helping customers with items on high shelves.

She stayed late, not going home until the doors were locked each night.

And Leo was still working as she left. Cleanup and restocking.

Thank god for computerized bookkeeping, else I'd be up till one in the morning!

She really wasn't surprised when the dog failed to come home Friday and Saturday nights.

Probably sleeping at the store, or someplace near.

God, Rachel, listen to yourself! The dog is out raiding trash cans, chasing cats, and looking for lady dogs in the mood to party. Leo, on the other hand, is sleeping wherever he lives.

At least I have Friday and Saturday off this week so I can relax.

And keep an eye on the dog.

Stone was still missing in the morning.

But he came back in time to watch the football game.

And eat pizza.

Chapter Twenty-four

Getting ready for the dance

I ran with Rachel Tuesday morning, then changed and headed for the bus stop.

This time I needed to be well north and hidden when the Hunters came.

If they came.

I mean, unless they were grabbing locals . . . my stomach clenched at the thought. But if they weren't grabbing locals, what were they doing out in the desert?

I didn't even know if they were going to the same place every time.

There was a war memorial just off the highway a quarter mile past the road they'd taken. I rested there. Snacked down on salami, cheese, and bread.

Much better than jerky.

I closed my eyes. And just sort of *felt* everything around. The memorial park, some kids playing basketball, a few houses. No Bad Guys.

I stretched and headed up the road.

Six miles to where it turned. I cut across open desert well before I got to the turn. Undressed and hid my clothes. Changed and trotted off northwest.

I didn't have a watch, but they showed up about when I expected them. Sick green auras, coming right at me. I ran away, trying to keep at the periphery of my ability to sense them—and presumably at the limit of them being able to sense me.

And then they weren't there.

I turned around and flipped a mental coin; angled north off the road.

Another mile and I could feel them again. I got nearer, stopped when I could sense individuals. A couple impatient and irritable. Old. Half a dozen youngsters, more anticipation than excitement. Hunger not yet pressing. But building.

The young ones were working under the direction of the elders. Clearing away brush.

Oh yeah. They're clearing a circle, like where they tried to kill me.

They're planning to kill someone.

One of the older Hunters is trying to teach them something.

The dancing ground. The chanting. Irritation rose.

I backed off to where I could barely feel them and waited

I remembered the Hunter, probably some cousin to some degree of mine, talking to Rachel. Following to find where she lived. My stomach clenched.

I have to talk to Kris. He's some kind of cop. Maybe a detective, he wears suits every day, and I can smell the gun oil, the leather, has to be a shoulder holster.

But will he believe me?

The sickly yellow-green glows, gathered together in three groups and started moving toward me. Since there was no reason to not believe that if I could see them, they could see me, I turned tail and bolted west into the desert. From what I hoped was a safe distance, I watched them drive back to the road and retrace their path. They turned toward Phoenix and sped up, disappeared beyond the limits of my odd "sight."

I turned and trotted back to where they'd been.

It was pretty obvious, from the ground. They'd parked on a slight slope, and over the crest, they'd cleared a circle of brush and rocks. And before they'd left, they'd dragged some dead mesquite back into the circle.

Hiding it from the air.

Two poles lay on the ground beside two holes dug into the sandy soil.

Poles. To tie their victims to. So they're planning on two victims?

They're all set up, whenever they want a dance. Do they work with the moon phases? I never noticed any difference. I suppose though, that it matters if you're driving across rough ground and don't want to show headlights.

I walked back to my clothes and curled up to sleep on them. The almost full moon rose before the sun set. If my memory of an astronomy class was right . . . tomorrow or the next day would probably be the full moon.

I'll go home tomorrow, warn Kris.

Somehow.

I have to trust him.

Chapter Twenty-five

Let's talk

Shit. This is going to be embarrassing.

Of course, if he is just a dog, he'll never tell anyone he was accused of being a werewolf.

If he even shows up tonight.

It was late when Kris got home. He sat in the car a moment, then repositioned the dash cam.

Nicole and Rachel were in the kitchen giggling as they cooked something that smelled fantastic. His guts unclenched.

Stupid idea. Really.

Nicole came out to give him a welcome home smooch. "If Rachel's going to keep that oversized mutt, we'll need a higher fence. Stone showed up in the back yard around noon, begging for food. He doesn't seem to be the least bit inconvienced."

Kris paused . . . and decided to not mention the wisdom of neutering . . . a possible werewolf. "Umm, yeah. So what smells so good?"

After dinner . . . he manufactured an excuse and invited Stone to take a ride.

Drove a few miles and pulled into a parking lot.

"Stone . . . we need to have a little chat. About what happened in Albuquerque." Kris turned and eyed the big dog in the back seat. "Or . . . do you prefer Leonard?"

The animal stiffened, backed into a corner.

And . . . his ears, smaller than most dog's, just the tips flopped over, shrank back against his head. And the muzzle, which had been more square than pointy was flatter and the hair seemed thinner . . . and there was a young man shifting around to sit like a human.

"Ow. That's not really fun, in case you wondered." The young man pulled what Kris had thought was a cloth collar over his head. He unclipped the dog tags and unrolled running shorts. Pulled them on.

"So what are you?"

"I'm not sure." The young man hunched his shoulders. "I was lost. Maybe my parents were killed. I don't know. I just . . . I was raised by some really great people. But they were old, and they died when I was in college. So I decided to try and find out who I was. Am. What I am."

"You didn't try before? Didn't tell the authorities?"

"I wasn't . . . I looked about five, I guess. But I wasn't actually talking, then. The Stones, they were my foster parents, they taught me to speak, got me up to speed that first year, so I could start first grade . . . Well, all I had were flashes of places, people I think were my parents, places they had been. After Mom died—my foster Mom—just a couple of weeks after Dad, I decided to try to find those places."

"Really?"

"Yeah. I'd been searching on the internet for years. So I went and found the zoo where that woman was frightened by the wolves. Found—I think—the Ferris wheel. Then I had a dream. It was rainy and cold and someone said 'I really miss the desert.' So I headed southwest."

"How'd you find them?"

"I . . . in Albuquerque, there was this restaurant. The waitresses kept looking at me, like they knew me and didn't particularly like me. I rented an apartment in the area. Ate there regularly."

His hands had been resting on the back of the

front seat. Now his head lowered and he rested his forehead on his hands. "Two men walked up . . . they looked a lot like what I see in the mirror. They asked all sorts of questions. And said someone must have gotten careless and let a woman live. They said I should come to the meeting . . . I was . . . scared . . . their eyes were . . . not friendly. But I had to go, I *had* to find out."

"There were a couple dozen of them there. At this big empty warehouse. Men. Some women back to one side, and a few kids. Dogs. Except they weren't really dogs." His voice got tight. "The leader, they called him Jack, said they were the hunters. The hunters of men and the devourers of souls. Sons of the Great Demon Sack a diffle or something stupid like that. The All-Mother who had given birth to their ancestors. 'The Four Sons of Men' they said, all deep and dramatic. I thought they were trying to fake me out, scare me or something."

Kris's fingernails bit into the palms of his hands, as he tried to not interrupt the flow of words.

"I . . . asked what they meant . . . what did they hunt? 'Humans,' they said. 'Women are the most fun,' some of them said. They were grinning and laughing. I laughed. 'Very funny, now what are you, what am I, really?' They laughed . . . and said this could be a good night for a hunt." He straightened, took a deep breath. "Join us or die. We'll kill tonight. You or another."

"I said hell no, tried to leave. They wrestled me down and tossed me in the trunk of a car. When they hauled me out, we were out in the desert, the sun just setting." He rubbed his forehead, stress lines across his forehead and showing in his voice. "There was a pole at one side of an open space. They tied me to it and started arguing, well, like they were *still* arguing about something. 'Wasting a consecrated dancing ground on a crossbreed' they said."

"The older ones said they ought to just kill me and what if the Great Demon didn't like being given a cross-bred descendant? The young ones said they'd found me and that they had the right to dance with the demon."

Kris's stomach was in a knot. *Demons on top of werewolves?*

"We're not werewolves. We're not even really dogs."

Kris froze . . . Coincidence or did he just read my mind?

"Anyway, the old guys said 'Go ahead, be fools' and they drove off. They left one car, the two guys from the restaurant and two of the dogs."

A couple of deep breaths, then the boy continued. "They sent the dogs off to collect firewood. Then they started a little fire from some dried brush and started dancing around it and singing . . . I've wondered about hallucinogenic herbs or mushrooms or something . . . between the smoke and the dust they were raising . . . I don't know what I saw, but I'd been changing, got my paws out of the ropes, started taking off my clothes. I can run much faster in dog form, but not when I'm trapped in a pair of jeans."

A long silence.

"They saw you . . . " Kris prodded.

"Yeah . . . are they dead? I just ran . . . didn't stop to check. Ought to have grabbed my clothes, or at least my wallet . . . and then the dogs found me. Fortunately just one at a time."

"Yeah. They're dead. Why didn't you go to the police?"

"I was too tired to change back. It takes so much energy, and I was hurt . . . I heal fast, especially in dog-form. But it was still five days before I could change."

"And by then, you'd hitched a ride down here, away from them."

He looked up, startled. "That was the idea, but they're here. In Phoenix. At least seven of them." He blinked. "But you're a cop, aren't you? You can take care of them, right? I know where those seven live."

Kris felt like he'd been sucker punched.

"How did you find them? Were you looking for them?"

The boy shook his head. "I spotted one . . . I didn't think he'd seen me, but . . . I was talking to Rachel. I left, thinking he hadn't seen me, but he went and talked to Rachel. And followed her home."

Kris froze.

"So I tracked him. There's three houses . . ."

Kris scrambled to grab a pad of paper and wrote down the addresses, asked for the address of the warehouse in Albuquerque . . .

"I tried to send that in anonymously, but nothing happened. They must have thought it was just a silly joke. There's a place in the desert I followed them to yesterday. They're getting a dancing circle ready. It's outside of Highway 303, north of Highway 60 about eight miles."

Kris swallowed. Had to reach for the professionalism that had become second nature. "I'll send this out . . . minus all mention of werewolves . . . Shit . . . and get Nicole and Rachel out of here for a few days . . . " He met the boy's eyes. "You can stay at the house. We may need your help. The mess in the desert? That was pure self-defense."

Leo shook his head. "It'll never come to trial. I'll stick around as long as I can, but I'm not going to disappear into some government laboratory."

"Umm . . . I . . . don't think we've got . . . anything like that." *Crap. I've fallen into a horror flick.*

The boy started laughing. "Maybe, maybe you should find out." He pointed at the dash cam. "Show them that."

"I'd rather just shoot myself." Kris sighed. "Right, so you can't change very often?"

"Not when I'm injured, dehydrated, and starving. Now? No problem. So if you don't mind? I'll just sack out in your yard and go to work early."

"Why there?"

"Because my first paycheck wasn't enough to rent even a cheap apartment, and everything I own is in

Albuquerque."

Including his wallet with his ID in the police evidence room there.

"Right. Back yard until I get the ladies someplace safe." Kris put the car in gear, and headed for the house.

He left the dash cam running, and presumably recording whatever Leonard Stone was doing in the back seat. When he pulled into the garage, it was a dog that jumped out of the back seat.

Nicole and Rachel were still up.

"Listen . . . " He trailed off. *How do you tell them a dog warned me . . .* "Umm, a case I'm working on has gone sideways, and there a good probability that they know who's investigating them. I was followed both away from here and back. I need both of you to leave, to go someplace safe for a couple of weeks."

Nicole looked worried, but Rachel was sitting up indignantly.

"I just started a new job. I can't go away for a couple of weeks!"

"It's . . ." Kris eyed the dog. *Stone will be there . . .* "I think you'll be fine so long as you stay away from here."

Rachel glowered, but reached for her laptop. "How about a hotel? There are some just off the freeway, maybe a mile . . . "

Stone interrupted with three sharp barks.

Kris eyed him, then turned back to Rachel. "Stone says three miles to be safe."

Rachel sputtered and Nicole laughed. "All right smart ass. For that, it'll be Wee Quiva."

Rachel eyed her.

"Upscale Hotel and Casino. We'll go in the morning, after the Bad Guys have followed Kris to the office."

Rachel typed away at her comp . . . "Ooo! Nice! There goes my first paycheck, which I haven't even got yet. I'll meet you there after work. Umm, do they allow pets?"

"Stone can stay here with me. And really, it should just be for a couple of days. I need to write some stuff up, if you two will excuse me?"

"Sure, no problem." The sisters exchanged glances and headed for the kitchen.

"God knows what the pair of them will cook up." Kris muttered, very quietly.

Stone thumped his tail, got up and followed the

women.

Kris stepped into the garage and pulled the chip from his dash cam.

I need this backed up, and a carefully cropped part of it sent to Dr. Reid. My Boss, the Albuquerque field office.

He fished Wright's card out of his pocket.

Yeah. Even Wright, this isn't the time for inter-agency rivalry. I'll have to say I let Leonard Stone get away. But we've got addresses. We know there are at least seven men here, a couple dozen in Albuquerque—plus women and dogs—so more of them . . . in dog-form.

But do we have enough evidence for warrants? For raids? Well, I can always arrest Stone.

Kris snorted. *He'd probably turn into a dog and woof at them, looking innocent. Dear God above, I'm going to wind up in the looney bin over this . . . nightmare.*

And I may have to actually ask someone if there's a "Really Weird Stuff" division tucked away somewhere.

He plugged the chip into his computer and copied it.

Sealed the original in an envelope and shoved it under other things in the top drawer. Cut the start and finish of the video.

This report is going to be . . . really interesting . . . even without the no fireworks, no eerie lighting effects Hollywood-does-it-better transformations.

The subject, Leonard Stone, see attached file 1, seems to believe he actually is a werewolf. The attached dash cam recording, see attached file 2, includes his claim of being the intended victim, and to killing both the men at the site, as well as two dogs.

No one is going to believe this. But with some careful surveillance to confirm . . . maybe we can wrap this up in a couple of days.

And they won't find Nicole or Rachel.

He choked, swallowed bile. Remembered what had been done to the Forty-eights' other victims.

I will watch Nicole leave in the morning. I will follow her, watch for anyone else following her. We'll all be fine.

Stone identified the following addresses . . .

Kris typed in the addresses both here and Albuquerque. Finished the report. Hesitated.

Sent it.

All Right, DOD. You've got your SWAT teams in Albuquerque? Take them out. A couple dozen men, Stone said. Plus women and dogs. Then get down here and deal with the seven Stone's found, and any others in their gang.

And hurry!

He didn't sleep well.

Got up in the middle of the night to open his gun safe and stare at his deer rifle. His larger caliber pistol. *Fast take down of a large dog. Or man. Hope I don't need silver bullets.*

He loaded both and put them—and extra ammunition—in the trunk of his car.

I'll remind Nicole to take hers.

***

Thursday morning he followed Nicole for two miles, then turned for the office.

For a frustrating morning trying to talk to anyone

in Albuquerque. "Thanks for the intel. We're too busy to chat. Go find Stone, I can't believe you let him get away, and stop bothering us."

Much peering at satellite photos, Google maps. Street views. Three houses in a row. landscaping no worse off than anywhere else in the desert.

The boss brought in sandwiches and they continued arguing, and watching the dash cam clip over again.

Masterson walked in, shaking his head. "We can watch them, but we can't do anything. Kris, I'll put people on Wee Quiva tonight."

Brad Cohen stopped the replay. "How'd he meet your sister?"

"They both work at Handyman Central on Bethany." Kris made a note. "I'll get, eventually, a warrant to see what employment history he gave them, what identification, since . . . well, the DOD by now, no doubt . . . has his wallet. Damn I'd like in on this."

He stared at the picture of the three houses. "Can we put a drone up to watch . . . "

Masterson was shaking his head. "I asked, and got an absolute no. The DOD owns this . . . operation."

Kris nodded. "I wonder if they're moving on them elsewhere? Get enough results and the announcement won't sound so bad. 'A Cannibal Cult that's been killing women all over the US for over a century and we've finally got some of them' is not going to be well received. 'Most of them' will pass muster."

His phone vibrated in his pocket. He got a censorious look, but pulled it out anyway. Unknown number.

"Hello?" He kept it neutral, uninformative.

"This is Stone. Rachel didn't come back from lunch, but her car is still in the parking lot."

Chapter Twenty-six

Search

"Nicole's phone is rolling straight to voicemail." Kris hoped he didn't sound as panicky as he felt. The conference room was silent.

He switched back to Stone. "When did she leave for lunch?"

"We do weird hours. I'm off 2 to 3, she's off 3 to 4. I didn't pass her when I got back, but it's a big store . . . I didn't realize she was still gone until I looked a few minutes ago, then looked for her car."

"Nicole's phone isn't . . . " *Working?*

"I'll head for those three houses. I can tell if she's there from two miles away . . . "

"Stay at the store, I'll pick you up. Fifteen minutes."

He was already on his way out the door. Masterson was a step behind him.

"Kris—do not go charging in and warn them—I'll get the PD's SWAT team moving."

Kris managed a nod as he hit the stairs. "Nicole

should have been at Wee Quiva. Get someone out to check."

Drove in cold fury, or perhaps cold terror.

At the store, Leo leaped in before he was properly stopped. "Go north on 43rd."

"I know where it is!"

"I just need to get within two miles . . . if they're not there . . . "

Kris swerved around a slow car, braked at a corner, looked, went, to hell with lights. Floored it and made a skidding left turn onto Northern on the yellow.

A quick glance at Stone as the boy's knuckles tightened. "They aren't there. No one's there. Get on 60 to the northwest. I've been tracking them. They went out into the desert a couple of times, that I know of. The last time I was out beyond Sun City when they turned off. I found where they went. I think they were setting up for their demon summoning."

Kris whipped onto the highway and sped up.

Reached and activated the phone system.

"Masterson? Stone says there's a spot in the desert they've been going to. I'm headed there right now . . . Stone, can you describe the place?"

"There's a road off Highway 60. It's after the overpass and before the Veteran's Memorial Park and it goes past a big development, fancy entrance, waterfalls and stuff. After five or six miles it bends left, two miles on, they drove off into the desert to the north."

Masterson's voice sounded irritated. "You couldn't get a street name?"

"It was one of these stupid number things. I was running. Hundred and sixty something."

And in the background "163rd. Goes past Asante."

"Masterson! Approach quietly! No helicopters until I'm on the ground. I'll sneak in close before the alarm goes up . . . " Kris shut up as Stone sat up in alarm.

"Outside of Albuquerque they started the ceremony when the sun touched the horizon, and said they had to finish just as the last of the sun dropped below the horizon."

Kris shot a glance at the sun, a hand width above the horizon, and concentrated on driving fast.

"Stone, get in the back seat and pull on those tabs to open it to the trunk. I think I want my guns up front."

Chapter Twenty-seven

Circle Dance

"If I were athletic, I'd sort of shimmy right up this pole and . . . and . . . you know, like Jackie Chan. He'd make it look like having his hands tied behind him was helpful." Rachel ran out of ways to try and talk herself out of a full-on hysterical breakdown.

It's only a few inches higher than my head. Jackie Chan would be up and out of here in ten seconds. But then he'd also beat up all twelve of these guys.

Three feet away, Nicole took a deep breath. "Kris was worried. They'll be looking for us."

"Right." Rachel stared at the dogs, running around, excited.

They look just like Stone. Well, lighter colored, but the same breed, obviously. Did my picking up a stray dog condemn my sister?

And the men. They all look so much alike. Like Leo.

No wonder he was afraid of his family.

They were in a low flat spot, a circle of sand and rock, cleared of the sparse brush. A few rocks around the boundary, probably also cleared out of the circle.

The cars were parked beyond the ridge, out of sight. No sign of civilization beyond their clothing.

One man bent and lit the kindling under the larger chunks of firewood.

And what's with the bonfire? Actually not that big of a fire. More family barbeque style.

What are they planning on cooking?

Rachel shuddered and did not speculate on what they had planned for after-dinner entertainment.

The sun was low . . . and suddenly every man and every dog went silent, facing the sunset.

The sun touched the horizon. A mass howl broke up into some wordless song, the dogs still howling as the men shouted. And danced and capered around the fire in an uncoordinated manner.

Shirts were being stripped off, one man pulled a long knife from the sheath on his belt. And danced around the fire, running the blade through the flame, and dancing off, touching first one man and then another with the knife. Running the knife through the flames, trailing smoke from burning blood Lines of red marked his passing and blood dripped down arms and was flicked into the fire.

Even the dogs ran up to be cut.

And some of the dogs convulsed . . . rolled on the ground howling in pain.

Rachel stared at one. Smaller than the rest. A paw, toes lengthening into fingers, muzzle pulling back into a human face . . . A young boy, howling and uncoordinated.

Oh. God. They really are werewolves.

A cloud of red smoke crept along the ground, and was carried aloft in the fire's draft. Tentacles of smoke, curling around dancing feet, drifting, rising, then blowing away in the faint cold breeze from the north. Getting nearer.

And the knife man danced toward them. Danced around them.

Rachel jerked her head around, trying to keep track of him.

The knife flicked out.

She jerked back, a stinging slash along her jawbone.

A wild ululation and knife man capered back to

the fire. A swing of the knife and red sparks flew when drops of blood hit the burning wood. Smoke billowed and rolled across the ground.

It's just smoke. . . really . . . The sunset's making it look so red, so solid . . .

Howls rose and the man with the knife turned, eyes fixed on Nicole.

Chapter Twenty-eight

Fight

"Lights, gun it. Hurry!" I pointed, leaning over the seat, and forced the words out as the change took hold. I braced myself, reached for the door latch as Kris floored the accelerator and snapped on the headlights. We zoomed between parked cars, went airborne as we crested the low ridge. I caught a brief glimpse of what I'd seen with my eyes closed. Poles on the right, fire to the left, men and dogs everywhere. One man near the women turning, knife in raised hand . . .

The car smacked down and skidded into the crowd, Kris twisting the wheel to break loose the rear and spin the car sideways into the middle of the dance.

I popped the door and charged the man turning toward Nicole, turning back, eyes widening as I leaped, body slammed him to the ground, teeth in his throat. A horrible gush of hot salty blood. I jerked back, jaws clenched and ripped his throat out. Twisted away and screamed as the knife hit my shoulder, scraped down the shoulder blade. I staggered away from the dying man, the knife clattered away and I jumped a dog heading for Rachel . . .

I could hear shooting, dodged the swipe of a clawed paw. *Oh claws, right.* I clenched my toes as I returned the swipe. The dog yelped, and I dived to rip at its throat. It turned and fled.

I vaulted to the hood of the car, pounced on the man coming up behind Kris. My jaws crushed bone and the hunter reeled away clutching his arm.

I spotted two men heading toward Rachel and charged at them with a roar worthy of a lion. Grabbed one by the shoulders, curled to get my hind legs up and clawed down his back and legs, dropped him and jumped the one turning back, a flaming firewood club swinging.

The dog-form was ill-suited for karate, but my reflexes got one foreleg up to save my head. I stood and chomped down on his face. Hard. Released him as he tripped and fell. Bolted behind Rachel, teeth to the rope holding her arms, then scramble to intercept a dog heading for Nicole . . .

Rachel threw herself forward, legs still tied to the pole, but she reached and grabbed the knife. She curled to slash the rope at her feet.

No shooting? I rounded the car to find a wrestling pile of men . . . I dived teeth first into a bare shoulder, rip the hunter out of the scrum. Leap on top of the struggling heap. Claws front and back, and two hunters turned to fight me.

Kris rolled loose, jumped for the car and grabbed the second pistol.

A yelp from the far side. I scrambled up and around. Nicole had the sacrificial knife in one hand and Rachel was swinging the flaming club at a dog. I leaped on top of it, jaws to the neck and felt it go limp as I severed its spine.

"Get in the car!" Kris yelled. Two more shots.

They dived for it. I body slammed a staggering bloody hunter . . .

Then the car was moving, jerkily, one tire burst, trailing oil. It stalled out at the edge of the circle.

And there was nothing between me and the fire. And the red smoke.

A curling tentacle . . .

I am imagining that, because of that story. I do

not believe in you.

I imagined laughter, words . . .

:: But I believe, and that is all that is needed. Come to me, Hunter, and I will show you pleasures beyond imagining. I will show you the greater Universe, things those little humans never dreamed of. Dance with me! ::

I shuddered and backed away, my eyes tearing in the smoke, making everything . . . strange.

"Stone!"

I jolted around, dodged the rock a Hunter tried to brain me with. Two more dogs rushing in.

Heard two snaps of a gun and one dog collapsed.

I leaped for the man. Took him down, but he grabbed my throat and started squeezing. I brought the claws into play and he screamed as blood flooded his face and I got the back claws into his belly and he flung me away.

The second dog was just a pup. It turned and fled.

I staggered, looked around. No one attacking. No one left to attack. I backed away from the smoke . . . the last of the sun sank from sight.

The car headlights came on.

There was no smoke. No voices.

160

I could hear more cars, and a helicopter.

Kris leaned into the car and grabbed his keys, stuff from the back seat, the rifle. "You two stay here. Stone, come with me, quickly." He led the way the rest of the way up the little ridge. Grabbed my ruff as I staggered up to the parked cars, and pulled me behind one.

Oh. Nicole's car.

Kris popped the trunk. "Get in. Otherwise someone's bound to shoot you." He threw his armful in.

I got my front end in. He grabbed and heaved the rest of me in. Closed me in. I heard his running footsteps, the cars, megaphones. Bright lights through every crack.

The cavalry had arrived. Probably just as dangerous to me as the Hunters. I put my head down and tried not to whimper in pain.

Chapter Twenty-nine

Debrief in the Desert

She was the last person to get treated. The . . . surviving werewolves had needed both lifesaving care and restraint. The guys in the DOD jackets, especially that Dr. Reid, had been positively gleeful at capturing some of the gang alive.

There was a helicopter circling the desert with a spotlight, looking for fugitives.

Stone, did you get away? Or, horrible thought! Did Kris take you out of sight and kill you?

There were lots of white sheets covering dead bodies. Human, and Canine.

Or are they all werewolves?

She and Nicole had been separated and questioned.

The kidnapping had been straightforward—she'd parked beside a tan van, gotten out of the car, the van door had slid and she'd been jerked inside.

What they'd wanted was the details of what they

called the dance.

Anything, any words, the rhythm.

She had a nasty feeling they wanted to give it a try.

Then she'd been left to wait for the medics to finish the more damaged. Including Kris. Who apparently knew the head DOD guy.

She eavesdropped shamelessly.

"The werewolves were fighting each other. I told you about Leonard Stone. Well, that's my best guess." Kris looked around at the carnage. "I hope . . . I suppose we won't know until the DNA results come back. Damn!" He wobbled a bit on his feet. His left arm was imitating a mummy and from what Rachel had seen there were a whole lot of stitches, possibly surgery and then a whole lot of physical therapy in his future.

"Right, well we caught one running away, but it was small. Four of the injured dogs are still alive, here, but they aren't friendly. And . . . Ah shit! Medic!"

Rachel jumped and grabbed as Kris folded.

But he didn't totally black out and the

overwhelmed EMTs stuck him in the front seat of the next ambulance to leave.

Then it was her turn.

Rachel held still while the medic cleaned her face.

"Just skin deep. I'll put butterfly tabs on it now, but they've got some really neat gizmos that'll do a better job, minimize scarring, so don't skip the ER." He looked over his shoulder. "We've sort of run out of ambulances for the moment."

"No kidding."

She'd listened, picked up bits and pieces, snatches of conversations, orders and reports. Something about "The Albuquerque pack," "heavy weapons," and "fire and explosion."

She could sort out Nicole's voice, still talking about her carjacking and kidnapping.

The medic sat back. "There you go. Remember, ER. Tonight. Well, technically, it'll probably be tomorrow morning before you get there. All we have to do is figure out *how* to get you there."

Rachel winced as she tried to smile. "Oww! Yeah, we used up a lot of ambulances. But Nicole's car is here, if they don't need it, maybe we can get ourselves there."

She stood up, the medic hovering as she wavered. She nodded that she was all right and headed for her sister, in amongst the mixed group of DOD, FBI, and a couple of boggled looking State Troopers who were being kept away from everything . . . odd..

Nicole grabbed her in a bear hug. Held her off to examine her cheek. "You need to see a doctor and I need to find Kris."

The head DOD guy frowned at them. "You understand you are not to talk about this?"

They both nodded.

Rachel looked at him. "Are you going to make most of this disappear? Turn it into, oh, I suppose a messy drug bust, and they had these vicious big dogs?"

His eyes narrowed. "Something like that. I would like to keep you two off the record."

"Well . . . Neither of us have filed police reports about kidnapping, or car hijacking . . . would it help to, umm take Nicole's car? Just drive away and we were never here? The car's parked up there . . . The keys . . . "

"Kris gave me his keys." Nicole dug in her pocket,

relaxed with a huff of relief as she pulled them out.

"An excellent idea." He checked something on his oversized phone. "Kovac's at Banner. Please drive carefully."

They staggered off, heading up the ridge.

"Nicole, are you all right to drive?"

"Yes. I'll be fine."

"Good, because I don't think I can and we really need to get out of here." Rachel collapsed into the passenger seat.

Nicole wound past a collection of vehicles and bumped carefully across the rough terrain, the route now well marked by crushed brush. The trooper at the road waved them on, phone to his ear.

"So. We've survived. Let's find Kris and get you seen by a real doctor."

Rachel nodded. "But first we're going home." *Surely they haven't bugged us?* "I'm going to take a shower."

"Oh, that sounds heavenly." Nicole turned onto the highway and sped up. "Home in twenty minutes."

Rachel nodded silently. *Please let me be right!*

She leaned her head back, a kaleidoscope of everything that had happened whirling through her head. She squinted at the dash . . . *less than eight hours. I came back from 'lunch' and that van parked beside me. I got out, the door slid open, and they pulled me right in.*

At least Nicole got as far as pulling her gun out of her purse. Pity she didn't shoot one of them. I wonder if I hit that dog hard enough . . . no, Stone got him. At least once he'd chewed through the ropes on my wrists I was able to get to the knife and free both of us.

She closed her eyes . . . blinked awake as Nicole pulled into the garage.

Swallow, straighten shoulders. "Pop the trunk."

She walked back and raised the lid.

He was there.

Limp and bloody, but looking at her. A soft thump of his tail . . . on his clothes.

Oh, that was what Kris got out of the back seat. Removing evidence that he was working with a werewolf.

That there was a werewolf who got away.

"Hi, Stone. Can you get out of there or should we take you to a vet . . . or a doctor?"

The big dog shoved himself up and oozed

carefully over the lip and down to the floor. Limped carefully for the door to the house. Nicole scurried ahead . . . by the time Stone had limped into the living room, Nicole had the back cushions off the couch, a blanket over them, a first aid kit . . . Stone limped past, and into the master bathroom's big walk in shower.

"Oh, good idea."

Rachel warmed up the water . . . with Stone opening his mouth to the spray and spitting . . . "Ew, yeah, you bit a lot of nasty . . . people, didn't you?"

"Here." Nicole pulled a new toothbrush out of a package, and supplied toothpaste.

But after getting his teeth—and the tongue he stuck out—brushed, Rachel carefully washed him down. All the blood on his face washed off, no sign of a bite or cut. *Not his blood.*

In fact, most of the blood proved to be not Stone's. A few claw trails, bites, and a single long deep cut down his shoulder. Still oozing, but not bleeding too much. She washed carefully around it, then flushed it out while he whimpered.

Dried him off, and applied antiseptics . . . "That cut ought to be stitched."

"Ger."

Rachel snorted. "That was the least threatening growl I've ever heard. But I'll leave it alone if that's what you want."

"Woof."

She grabbed a towel and started rubbing where he wasn't injured.

"Do you need anything to eat? Or . . . "

"Woof!"

Nicole snickered. "Right, how about some soup . . . "

Then he limped to his improvised bed and stretched out.

Rachel covered him up. "Okay, we're going to shower, and then I need to see a doctor. And Nicole needs to check on Kris."

Thump, thump.

He was snoring when she walked back downstairs.

Chapter Thirty

All done but . . .

Kris hurt everywhere.

The doctor cheerfully informed him he'd lost track of the count of sutures around a hundred and fiftyish, but not to worry. The ones that couldn't be seen would dissolve, and he could see his regular doctor about removing the surface stitches in ten days and get recommendations for physical therapy.

"To rehab all those muscles I just stitched back together. The rest is just bruises. You did a good job protecting your head." The doctor sighed then. "I really wish your scary DOD buddies would tell me what happened."

Kris just grunted. "The DOD has . . . the mindset of keeping everything secret. Interagency rivalry being what it is, even I won't get details. Stupid. It was 'just,' if I can use the term, a big drug bust gone tits up, with a boatload of vicious trained attack dogs. The main problem—the drug gang managed to offload most of the drugs somewhere else, so the DOD is pissed that they've got to run off and figure out where it all went. And don't want to admit to the DEA that they lost track of it."

And that's the official story that will be allowed to leak a bit, then reluctantly admitted to. Damn Wright. They had the three house addresses and botched the surveillance. They all got away, and headed straight for Nicole and Rachel.

A tap at the door, Nicole peered in.

The doctor looked relieved. "You must be Mrs. Kovac. Good. Here are the prescriptions. Instructions. I doubt you'll have any trouble keeping him in bed for a few days, but try to make him take it easy for at least a week. I'll see him then—call my office for an appointment—then if he's doing well, his regular doctor can take over."

Nicole gulped a bit, looking him over. "Well, I put Rachel to bed, and fed the dog. All that's left is to get you home."

The dog. Excellent.
I think.

He stumped carefully in from the garage and

grinned at the sight of the big dog under one blanket on the floor and his sister-in-law wrapped in another blanket on the couch. Neither of them stirred as they passed. He eased into the kitchen.

Nicole shook her head. "I'd kiss you if I could figure out where it wouldn't hurt. And would you like breakfast, or would you like some soup like your fellow hero?"

"Soup sounds like a good idea." He eyed her worriedly.

She snorted. "This wasn't your fault, or even your job's fault. It doesn't really even have anything to do with Stone. They were babbling things like what strong auras we had, when they'd seen us, they had to have us and so forth. Maybe Stone can explain, when he changes back . . . he will change back, right?"

"I think so. He said the last time he was injured it was five days before he could change again, so don't expect anything soon. Oh, and he may not know. I was investigating him." Kris looked around as Rachel trailed in, yawning. "He was orphaned or abandoned when he was five years old, raised by some nice, elderly foster parents. Meeting his blood relatives . . . has no doubt been a bit of a shock."

Rachel nodded. "He was terrified of them . . . I figured he was a coward. Or he'd done something horrible that his family rejected him for. Oh brother, did I get that all wrong."

Nicole shivered and leaned carefully on Kris's right shoulder—the one without stitches. "I had no idea . . . things like that were real."

Kris nodded. "Me neither, and in three weeks I'll probably decide it was all a drug induced hallucination. Except, well, Stone."

Rachel nodded. "Are they, I mean, those DOD guys who told us to never talk about it? What will they do with Stone? Or to him?"

"I don't know." Kris looked toward the sleeping werewolf. "He may need to quietly leave the area."

***

"Mexico might be your best bet." Kris eyed the young man, sitting so uncomfortably on the couch.

"No passport, and yes, I could just trot across the border. But while I speak Spanish, I'll never pass as a native. All things considered, I'd rather stay in the US."

Kris eyed the books on the table. "Nothing on werewolves?'

"I've read everything ever written, over and over. As far as I can tell, it's all hogwash." The young man crossed his arms and thrust his jaw out stubbornly. "I don't believe in magic."

Kris sighed. "Leo . . . you're a werewolf."

"Dog. Sort of a dog. With lion claws. Doesn't mean there's not a scientific explanation. I see no reason to believe in demons and . . . things."

"You saw the same thing I saw."

"I breathed the same nasty smoke you did. Some hallucinogen. Just suggestion and smoke. I have no interest in pursuing the least sensible idea. I need to get somewhere, find a new job, get back to work and just be normal." He bit his lip. "Do you know anything about them? I . . . nothing ever leaked about actual . . . weird stuff?"

"The only weird I knew about was that the DNA traces from victims at every site had two extra chromosomes. We called them the Forty-eight gang."

"I see . . . *every* site? How many . . . how long has this been going on?"

"The oldest kill site we've found is over a century old. Okay, no DNA evidence from the oldest sites, but the rest of the evidence fits. Thirty-five sites, the remains of a hundred and two women and two men."

"Err . . . "

"Not counting the two bodies between Albuquerque and the Arizona state line." Kris sighed. "I worked the sites on either side of the North and South Carolina border. There's a cluster in Upstate New York . . . Were you in Maine?"

"And New Jersey and Connecticut. I found a couple of places I sort of remember from when I was little. Then I had a dream about a woman—I've dreamed her before. I think she was my biological mother. In the dream she said "I miss the desert." So I decided to head for Texas and see if anything stirred up any memories."

"Did it?"

The young man shook his head. "So I kept going. To Albuquerque. They spotted me in that restaurant I told you about. Or maybe they can see me the way I can see . . .feel . . . them."

"From two miles away, you said?"

"Almost three." He started looking cautious. "You said four clusters?"

"Southern California through Phoenix—and now extending into Albuquerque. And the Pacific

Northwest."

"Is there anywhere that you've never heard of their activity?"

Kris shrugged. "They've got both coasts pretty well covered, but the middle . . . Denver, maybe?"

"Oh, that would work. I'd just need to get there without going through Albuquerque. Although I'd like to pick up my car."

"I don't know if the DOD is watching the airport here. But I can drive you to Tucson." Kris pulled out the pre-paid credit card. "I owe you a hell of a lot more than a plane ticket."

"Oh. But . . . won't they trace it? The DOD?"

"They may. There are no guarantees in life."

"Right." Leo looked beyond him.

Rachel walked down the last three steps. "You can't stay, can you?"

Leo met Rachel's gaze. "I don't dare."

Kris looked back and forth between them . . . got up and left quietly.

***

Rachel sat down beside him. "I . . . Leo? Umm . . . "

There was sad acceptance in his eyes. "Rachel . . . I'm not close enough to normal myself to ever dare . . . a normal life . . . with, umm . . . "

"A wife. Children . . . I don't know if I'd dare have half-werewolf children."

"I don't know what they'd be like. Maybe the DOD can figure it out from the . . . people they captured. Of course they'll never tell us." Leo smiled wryly. "So why don't we just be friends, until I leave, which I probably ought to do fairly soon."

"Yeah, you know, you're a really nice dog and a nice person."

He grinned. "I like to think of myself as a person with both a human-form and dog-form. There's no . . . wild beast instincts taking over like in the movies. I hate werewolf movies. And it's not contagious. I think it must be genetic."

"I'm afraid to ask how you know that."

"Mom and Dad—my foster parents—said we had to know. They argued for a week over which one ought to be bitten, because the other one had the moral fortitude and ability to rid the world of the menace and so forth. And another week before I nipped Mom. And she scolded me and made me really bite her. I ran outside and barfed, at the taste of blood. Nothing happened. Then Dad talked me into biting him, just in case it only infected men. Nothing."

Rachel was stifling giggles.

"Yeah, It was pretty funny, afterwards. It was actually a relief." I leaned my head back and stared at the ceiling.

My relatives are not my problem! The FBI and those DOD guys can deal with them!

My problem is this gorgeous blonde leaning in for a kiss.

"I have to leave." I stumbled to my feet. "I have to." I turned and walked out the back door to collect the rest of my clothes.

***

Kris eyed Wright. "You want me to take over all the investigation and clean up for both Albuquerque and Phoenix areas? Everything?"

Wright nodded . . . gritted his teeth. "Agent Kovac, much though it pains me to say this, my small group has spent the last twenty years investigating UFOs, Bigfoot sightings, crop circles, and chupacabras. As you might well imagine, this was considered a punishment assignment, and a place to put the politically incorrect agents. Fortunately, no seriously incompetent people. And real, actual, werewolves has us scrambling for personnel, not to mention facilities for our captured werewolves."

Kris paused . . . "Yes . . . I guess finding out you weren't a joke has been . . . interesting. How many werewolves did you capture?"

"Five dogs and seven men and boys who are sometimes human and sometimes canid. And six women we managed to track down when one returned to the houses we had under surveillance for something she'd left behind. Apparently none of them can change, but they've all got one or the other of the extra chromosomes. You and your buddy Leo killed nine and wounded eight. We found four more out in the desert and captured them."

Wright scowled. "So we're pretty busy, and really short on trained, experienced, investigators at the moment. And while we can request assistance of any of the various agencies . . . we really would prefer someone who already believes in werewolves."

Kris sighed. "All right, but only temporarily. Then I'm getting back to plain old crime."

Chapter Thirty-one

Not the future I'd planned

I'd only lived in Albuquerque a week. I'd stayed two days in a motel, then rented a grubby efficiency in a poor part of town. The biggest surprise was that my car was still there.

It was no problem getting into the apartment—years of unexpected changes had trained me in redundancy—the spare door key was where I'd left it, the car keys were where they'd been hidden inside.

Well, everything I owned fit right back in the six boxes I'd taken them out of . . . had it really been less than a month? I wasn't even late on the rent.

I humped the boxes out to the car, rolled up the futon and dumped it on the backseat.

Straightened to eye the man leaning on a post, watching me.

He shoved off the post and walked closer. "Moving again, Mr. Stone?"

"Yes." I eyed him. *Government. Crap.*

"Los Angeles is beautiful in the fall." He dipped his fingers into his shirt pocket. "Call me when you find your family again."

"I was hoping to avoid them."

He held out an envelope. "We need to find them. Stop them."

Oh Shit.

I'm neither a hero nor a cop.

Yet.

I reached out and took the envelope.

Excerpt from the next Stone story

Los Angeles was a smoky mess in the Fall.

The Santa Ana winds were whipping wildfires down canyons and burning homes. Just like most years.

It seemed like I heard about the fires every year . . . you'd think by now they'd have run out of things to burn. But then people are stubborn, and do tend to rebuild after disasters, instead of sensibly relocating. At any rate, the traffic was hideous, the roads in need of repair—what the heck were they spending all the gasoline tax money on, anyway?

I followed the directions and found the address on the, well, I wasn't sure if they were orders or suggestions, yet. But they said to go to the office and introduce myself. I had expected an office building, and gotten apartments.

I parked in a visitor's slot and headed for the office to see what I'd let myself in for.

I tapped at the door marked office and tried the knob, walked in.

The . . . person . . . at the desk glowered in my general direction. Quite an impressive expression, what with the rings and studs and tattoos and purple hair.

"Hi. I'm Leo Stone . . . "

A grunt. The person dipped down behind the desk and emerged with a manila folder.

"Sign here. There's a dripping faucet in the bathroom. It's on the list. It'll get fixed next week."

"Right." I looked over the papers . . . apparently I'd already paid in full for a three month rental, plus a hefty cleaning deposit. I grabbed a pen from amongst the random clutter of the desk and signed. "I can probably fix the faucet myself."

That got me a skeptical look. "Right, like a Mooovie Starrrr knows plumbing."

I glanced back at the papers. Sure enough, occupation actor.

Whatever. "Well, you never know what you'll wind up doing, do you?"

He . . . or she or xee or whatever . . . handed me three keys on a ring with a paper label that bore a 321.

"You lock yourself out, it's a five dollar charge for me to come open it up. And ten if I have to replace the key, twenty if I have to replace the lock. The post office charges fifty if you lose the key to your mail box."

"Thanks, umm, where . . . "

It pointed. "Stairs. Third floor, turn right."

"Right. And parking . . . "

"They're numbered. Don't park in anyone else's space."

"Right. Thank you."

"Eh."

Nice friendly people, these Californians.

It only took two laps of the parking lot to find slot 321, in an awkward dead end.

I slung my backpack over my shoulder and hauled a box of books out of the trunk of the car.

There was a sort of tunnel through to a small courtyard that was mostly swimming pool. The tunnel held the stairs, and the mail boxes.

I headed up the stairs. Eight days was really not long enough to recover from the fight I'd been in . . . I was whimpering a bit by the time I got to the third floor and turned right down a passage with doors on both sides. Apartment 321 was the first door to the right, the side away from the courtyard and pool. Could it possibly have a view? The key got me into a musty shadowy room. I nudged the box over the threshold and walked around opening curtains. All two of them. But the sliding glass doors led to a small balcony with a view of trees and through them, what looked like another apartment building. The tiny kitchen took up one corner of a room that would serve as dining, living and bed room, and a tiny bathroom tucked behind the staircase.

"Mr. Wright, you're a cheap bastard. It's perfect."

I opened the window and sliding glass door so musty could be exchanged for smoky and hot. Rotated my right shoulder carefully—owwww!—and headed down to fetch more boxes.

By the time I staggered up the stairs with my last load—futon and pillow—my right shoulder was screaming.

"Dude, you're bleeding."

I staggered around in a half-circle to see who was talking.

Big beefy black guy, standing in the door across from mine. Mild expression, t-shirt, jeans, flip flops. A can in each hand.

"Drat. Knew I should have gotten stitches. Oh well." I unlocked the door again and staggered through.

"Hey, do you mind? I always wondered what these efficiencies were like . . ."

Oh bloody hell the friendly type. He's following me.

". . . Oh, I see, the bathroom's back there, and the staircase is where my bedroom is. I'm Wally."

"Leo."

"Oh good, that beats Lenny. I've hated every Lenny I've ever met."

"Umm, I take it Mr. Purple in the office talks a lot?"

"Mister . . . " Wally snickered, coughed, gave up and cackled. Panted and cleared his throat. "Miss Wintrope thought I would find having a fellow actor for a neighbor a refreshing change."

He held out a can—ah a cold coke. I could get to like a neighbor like this.

"Miss. Right, well it was hard to tell." I popped the tab and look a chug, which gave me enough time to decide to not ask what style of plumbing Miss Purple had and whether it was original or surgical.

"Leo Stone . . . not a bad name. Is it your real one? I'm officially Wallace Carson McBride. I've tried to think of something better, but I just wind up with silly D and D style things."

"Fleet Sword Smighter and so forth?"

"Not quite that bad."

"Carson's a good strong name. You could go a bit ethnic, everything's so PC these day's you should give it a try."

He nodded thoughtfully. "Carson Chan."

I snorted coke.

The Hunters of Men will be available in the fall of 2019

Excerpt from Book One of the Wine of the Gods

Outcasts and Gods
Pam Uphoff

18 May 2111

"I rule the world!" Wolfgang Oldham whipped the interface helmet from his head and fell over onto his back. "I am all powerful! Fear me!" He gathered a glowing ball of fire between his hands.

"I'm terrified, dear. Have you done your homework?"

Wolfgang grinned up at his mother. She couldn't see the fire at all. Even the twins could just barely see it in the dark. "All done before I even made it home. I hope college is more challenging than high school." He put a hand down casually, off the rug, onto the limestone tiled floor and let the energy seep into the ground.

"I suspect so, and while you're unplugged, why don't you run check the mail. We ought to be getting replies back from colleges soon."

"Yes, ma'am, sir, ma'am!" He jumped to his feet, saluted and galloped out the door. "Please, please, please. West Point. I want to go to West Point like Dad." He kept his voice down so the neighbors wouldn't think he was weird. Weirder.

Of course he'd applied at other places as well, but he'd made no bones about his favorite. Nothing, though. Well, something from Healthy Kids. He eyed it dubiously. Not more tests! Once a year was *enough* and anyway, he was sixteen. A year and a half away from official adulthood.

He peeled it open and read it as he walked back inside.

"Ugg, Mom, Healthy Kids wants me to come in for some more tests. Gotta get their last vials of blood before I fly the coop."

"I hope they don't expect you to miss any school." Mom was in full cooking mode now, green apron clashing with maroon kitchen, three pots on the stove. Chicken, green beans, potatoes.

The twins came tearing through the door, laughing and talking about something that had happened at soccer practice. They were his parent's real kids. Some of the first ever vat grown, because of the problems his mother had, but still ninety-nine point nine percent genetically theirs. At least they'd chosen the same two standard suites of selected genes that he had, so the twins were sort of barely related to him. They hadn't gone for the two special suites, which, no matter how much he wished he had someone he could talk to about it, he did understand. Thirteen years ago the test kids with those special suites had become political hot potatoes.

If only the sensation seeking media hadn't started calling them "gods" it wouldn't have been so bad. Or at least the foaming-at-the-mouth churches wouldn't have taken them up as the latest thing to try to have destroyed.

If only society weren't so anti-children. worldwide, the reproduction rate was well below replacement level, it was crashing in most of the West, but still people carried on about overpopulation.

His father followed the twins through the door; he always picked them up after soccer practice, and Tilda after piano lessons and Markly and Wolfgang after karate . . . He had the best parents in the world. Hands down. No matter what names the "child free" called them when they were out in public with three children. "Breeders" and "Parasites."

His father glanced through the mail and tossed half of it. He read through the letter from Doctor Winston. "Well, we shouldn't begrudge them a bit of blood now and then. They did a damn good job on you. But you must be sick and tired of all this."

"Oh, well, yeah, but the talk about frankensteins is back again, and the President's speech last week . . . We need to demonstrate that we're dedicated to helping everyone." Wolfgang shrugged, trying hard not to show what a shock that speech had been. *He said that being made artificially, that having animal genes, we didn't have souls. Right. Two or three genes out of tens of thousands . . . a gene complex for a pigment. Blue pigment from a freaking bird, so with a bit of tweaking with some other genes they can make kids with blue or purple hair.*

His father squeezed his shoulder. "You're taking it better than I ever would have. That man just lost a hell of a lot of votes in the Milwaukee region."

Wolfgang closed his eyes and could still see the glows of his family. The twins were the brightest. The other Test Kids he'd met at the clinic on occasion had had even brighter glows. He wondered what the glows were, and why he could see them. Auras? Magnetic fields generated by the nervous system? Like the fire-ball-that-wasn't-there, it had all started happening last year when his body had finally decided it was time for puberty.

"Anyway, Doctor Winston wrote a note that he was holding a spot open for Friday at six PM. I'll just take the bus down after school and get it over with."

Maybe ask some questions.

194